A MONSTER WORTH FIGHTING FOR

Monster Between the Sheets, Season 2

Ava Ross

A MONSTER WORTH FIGHTING FOR

Monster Between the Sheets, Season 2

Copyright © 2023 Ava Ross

Cover art by Clover Book Cover Designs

Editing/Proofreading by JA Wren & Owl Eyes Proofs & Edits

*For my parents who
always believed I could do this.*

Series by AVA

Mail-Order Brides of Crakair

Brides of Driegon

Fated Mates of the Ferlaern Warriors

Fated Mates of the Xilan Warriors

Holiday with a Cu'zod Warrior

Galaxy Games

Alien Warrior Abandoned

Beastly Alien Boss

Bride of the Fae

A Sci-Fi Holiday Tail

Monsterville, USA

Monster on Board
(co-written with Alana Khan)

A Monster Worth Fighting For
(Monster Between the Sheets)

Love at First Orc

Third Galaxy on the Left

You can find her books on Amazon.

A Monster Worth Fighting For

**Grumpy, growly wyverns don't deserve
true love
—or do they?**

I've worked hard to accept what happened after I sipped that strange brew and turned into a wyvern. Scaly skin? It protects me from the weather. Wings? Flying's cool. And the claws on my thumbs make it easier to craft chainsaw wood sculptures.

But then Nettie, a too-adorable woman with curves that go on forever and long hair the color of the sunset, arrives on my doorstep.

She insists we were married by proxy. Thanks for asking me to sign those papers, Mom.

When a freakish storm hits the area, we're stuck together trying to figure this out. Did I mention my log cabin only has one bed?

My lonely heart keeps insisting I should keep her, but what woman wants to be a wyvern's bride?

A Monster Worth Fighting For is part of the Monster Between the Sheets Season 2. Each standalone book features a different monster and is full of heat, humor, and comes with a HEA guaranteed.

Who says monsters can't fall in love? In Screaming Woods, anything is possible. Welcome back to the little town turned monstrous by a party potion gone wrong. Your favorite instalove authors are bringing you hairier, scarier, and hornier monsters than ever before in this beastly series coming to your kindle now.

Chapter 1
Nettie

I couldn't believe I'd talked myself into being a wyvern's mail-order bride. Yet, here I was, on a one-way trip to move in with my new husband. We were married by proxy two days ago, after which I packed my few possessions, snuck out of my controlling father's house, and boarded a plane to Screaming Woods, a tiny town where monsters were created.

I hadn't met my husband, though we'd chatted a lot via email, but I knew what he looked like. I'd dog-eared his grainy photo, studying it thousands of times after I'd accepted his proposal and agreed to say I do. Tall, he had glorious copper-colored wings and a handsome face. It was the hint of loneliness in his dark eyes that drew me in because it mirrored the feeling inside me.

Frankly, when I saw his post on the dating site, I laughed. Who'd agree to become a monster's mail-order bride sight unseen?

My laughter had faded fast when my father called

me downstairs and announced he was marrying me off to one of his business associates who had to be three times my age. Dad owed the guy money, and I was the payment.

Absolutely not.

"I won't do it," I told him, lifting my chin. My heart cringed. *I* cringed because I knew standing up to him would get me nowhere. From the time my mother died when I was eight, he'd ruled over me with a strong will and an iron fist he used once too often.

That's when I started pouring over the Bride Wanted ads online. Most, I dismissed, because it was clear they'd been posted by creeps. But the small ad for someone to marry a wyvern and move to his cute little cabin in the woods in a town where monsters were created kept drawing my eye.

I filled out the application, and my now-wyvern-husband, Ryett, had reached out. We'd chatted back and forth through email until he told me he thought we'd fit well together.

"Almost there," the Lyft driver said, squinting at me in the rearview mirror. He'd taken me from the airport along winding roads, then through the center of Screaming Woods, a sweet little town surrounded by dense forest. "Are you sure you don't want me to take you back to the airport? A big storm's coming, but I bet you could get a flight out before it hits. It's not too late." He frowned, and his voice dropped. "I can't imagine leaving a tiny little thing like you deep in the woods when it's going to rain cats and dogs. Lots of wind expected, too, plus power outages."

I wasn't worried about the storm. Ryett would make sure I was safe.

"My husband's waiting," I said, grinning like I had each time I whispered the title since I'd married him in a proxy wedding.

In one of our final emails, he told me he would give us time to get to know each other before asking for anything else. What a complete gentleman. I pictured a shy, sweet guy who was polite and who'd care about my needs as much as his own.

While I might be a silly, sheltered woman, I'd already half-fallen for him in my dreams. He was so generous he'd paid for my flight and sent me money not only to buy new clothing but to use during my travels.

I suspected it wouldn't be hard to slip into my dream image's bed and be with him forever.

With a neutral grunt, the driver took the vehicle up a long dirt driveway and parked in front of a log cabin with a big deck spanning the front. Squinting out the left window, I took in the view of mountains in the distance and the picturesque town nestled in the valley, though angry clouds loomed over everything. Despite the incoming storm, summer had arrived in this part of the world, and bright green leaves covered the trees, contrasting nicely with the darker evergreens. In winter, everything must be incredibly pretty covered in snow; I couldn't wait to see it.

Me and Ryett would stomp through the snow and

select a tree to cut for the holidays. We'd buy or make our own ornaments, then hang them together, teasing each other and sharing kisses.

I was getting ahead of myself, but almost from the moment I'd seen his ad, hope for a bright, loving future had filled my heart to overflowing. He'd step in and fill the place left gaping after my mother's death.

It started sprinkling, and the driver turned on the car's wipers, making a swish-slap, swish-slap sound echo in the small space.

After he put the vehicle in park, he watched me through the rearview mirror as I got out, dragging my solitary bag with me. Rain and wind hit me, but I wouldn't be dissuaded. My new, wonderful life was about to begin, and a bit of bad weather wouldn't hold me back.

I leaned inside and shot the driver a grin. "Thank you. I appreciate the ride."

"You take care, little lady." He nodded and frowned, shooting a gaze toward the sturdy wooden cabin that would soon be my home.

Once I'd shut the door and started slogging through the growing puddles and sheets of rain toward the building entrance on the right side, the driver turned and took the vehicle back down the drive, soon disappearing into the storm.

Only a hint of trepidation shot through me as I climbed the back steps up to the deck and approached the door. Mostly, I was incredibly excited.

I'd evaded my father's trap, marrying who *I* chose.

He couldn't force me into an unwelcome marriage any longer.

I lowered my bag onto the deck and shoved my already saturated hair off my face, wishing I'd pulled it up into a ponytail. But it was my best feature, long and auburn, and my mom once told me never to cut it. I had to eventually, but it still swept across my lower back.

I opened the outer door, studying the hand-hewn wooden panel with a dragon carved into the center. No, a *wyvern*. Its craggy face was highlighted by majestic horns, and its glorious wings spread out in welcome.

Did the creature resemble my husband? That could be why I was nervous. I knew a person's insides were what mattered, but what would it be like to be married to a man who looked like a mythical creature?

I'd looked up wyverns online. A two-legged, winged creature with a pointed tail. His picture showed two sharp horns curving up over his head, copper, lightly scaled skin, brown hair brushing his muscular shoulders, and claws on his thumbs—though he'd told me once he didn't have them on his fingers. A ridge of flexible spikes jutted down his spine. I'd only seen the shadow of those in the picture, and I imagined they could tighten if he needed them for defense.

I couldn't tell from the picture if he breathed fire or had fangs, because he was gazing solemnly at the camera.

I was about to find out.

"Knock on the door," I whispered. "Meet him. He said he'd give you an annulment if we didn't mesh." But in my heart, I knew we were the right match. I'd known it from the moment I spied the stark sadness in his dark eyes that matched the feeling within me.

Lifting my shaky hand, I knocked on the door.

I fidgeted on the brush mat, trying to ignore the rain drizzling down my spine.

He knew I was coming. He said he'd be waiting. My silly, romantic heart had pictured him meeting me at the door with a bunch of wildflowers in his hand. He'd smile and tug me inside, showing me his home, and then sit me down at the kitchen table where we'd share the meal he'd prepared to celebrate our marriage. There would be candles, more flowers on the table, and he'd tell me he was incredibly happy I'd arrived. We'd talk, bond, and things would only get better after that.

I rapped my knuckles on the door again. Perhaps he was busy getting dinner ready and hadn't heard me knock.

The panel was wrenched open, and Ryett stood in the opening, scowling.

"Hi," I said in a shaky voice. "Hi, Ryett. I've arrived."

A growl ripped up my new husband's throat and a blast of smoke shot from his nostrils. "Who the hell are you?"

Chapter 2
Ryett

A delectable, curvy little redhead stood on my deck, soaking wet to the bone and beyond bedraggled. She gazed at me with hope and excitement in her pretty brown eyes.

My tail whipped back and forth behind me, showing my agitation.

"I'm your wife, Nettie," she said in a trembling voice.

"I don't have a wife," I snarled. What kind of joke was this? I leaned around her to peer outside, noting no other vehicles in the driveway. "How in the hell did you get here?"

"I took a Lyft from the airport." She swallowed hard and her lower lip quivered before she shored it up with a tightening of her spine. "Did I arrive on the wrong day or at the wrong time?"

"What are you talking about?"

"I'm Nettie. You're Ryett." Her voice came through strong despite my growls and smoke. I had to hand it to her; this female had spunk. "I replied to your ad for a mail-order bride, and we've talked via email for months. We were married by proxy two days ago." Her big eyes with incredibly long lashes pinned me in place. "The papers are in my bag." She waved to it sitting by her feet, as saturated as her by the storm. "Surely you haven't forgotten all about it?"

For whatever reason, my mind shot to the papers my mother brought by for me to sign a few weeks ago. She'd thrust them in front of my face when I was busy crafting my latest commissioned chainsaw carving—a crouched bear—and stated they related to the estate my great-aunt had left me when she died. She gave me the almost five hundred acres surrounding the log cabin I'd built with my own two hands—and claws. I'd thought nothing of it, signing the papers quickly before returning to work.

Mom had given me an odd smile afterward, but I'd dismissed that too.

"Mom," I bellowed, but it was useless to yell. She'd remain well away from the scene of the crime. I scowled at Nettie. "You need to leave."

Her eyebrows lifted. "No, I need to come inside. I'm wet. I'm getting cold. And the driver has left." Her bag in hand, she nudged past me, stepping into my small entry, where she peered around.

For some reason, I saw everything as she must. Butcherblock counters I'd crafted myself, sanding and coating them with poly until they gleamed. A black cast iron sink that matched my appliances.

Rough floorboards that still needed another coat of poly. I'd planned to do that this summer.

"I'm still working on the place," I said, hating that I made excuses to . . .

No!

She was not my wife.

"It looks nice," she said softly. "Comfy."

Her appreciation of my home shouldn't please me. Neither should the curvy shape she revealed when she took off her coat, carefully draping it over the back of one of the chairs in front of the kitchen island.

She had big boobs and a great ass—I shouldn't notice that, either.

"Let me grab those papers." She dug around in her bag and pulled them out, though I didn't have to look. I'd signed them; I was confident about that. Any judge worth their weight would agree I'd done so without full knowledge. We could end this before it got started, and I could go back to my solitary life deep within the forest.

"I don't need a wife," I said, glancing down at the papers before nudging them back her way. Yeah, my signature was scrawled across the bottom. "It appears there's been a mistake."

Her heartfelt sigh stabbed through me like a blade. Why did I care about her feelings? I didn't know her, and despite how attractive I found her, I didn't care.

"My mom made me sign some stuff a few weeks ago," I said, sharing my suspicion.

One of her auburn eyebrows lifted. "Made?"

"Asked. Same thing."

She blinked slowly before her eyes widened. "You mean I've been corresponding with your mother all this time?" she barked. "Shit, shit, shit." She stomped back and forth in front of me, dripping water all over the floor. "It was you."

"I didn't email you."

"Someone did!"

"My mother," I growled. Damn her.

Lightning crackled overhead, followed by a big boom of thunder. The storm of the century had arrived, and it would deluge us for the next few days if the weatherperson was to be believed. Something about it stalling overhead.

"I can't believe I half fell in love with your *mother*." Stopping in front of me, Nettie gave me a glare worthy of . . . *me*, actually.

Yeah, I was cranky. I had good reason to be.

"You don't love me," I snarled.

Her lips twisted. "Evidentially, I don't even know you."

"My mom's already married."

"I can't believe this." She growled; a sound almost worthy of me. "I guess we'll have to get a divorce or an annulment, then." Tears filled her eyes, and her shoulders sagged. "I'm not going back to my father." Despite her drooping posture, her chin lifted. "He's got some rich old guy in mind for me to marry as payment for a debt. I don't even know him, though I don't know *you* either. Still, I won't do it."

Hell, no. I might not want Nettie, but I didn't want

her marrying some rich dude for . . . "Did you say to settle a debt?"

"Yeah." Her pretty features twisted. "Crappy thing to do to your daughter, right? It wouldn't be the first horrible thing he's done to me, however." After donning her coat and grabbing her bag, she eased around me and opened the door. "Sorry to have bothered you. I'll find my way to town. Is there a bus station nearby?"

Maybe. I didn't know.

Rain pelted Nettie, my floor, and a gust of wind knocked her backward. Before she could step outside, I snagged her arm, holding her back.

I slammed the door and, lifting her, placed her in one of the island chairs. Damn, she was tiny.

She felt too good in my arms. Smoke coiled from my nostrils, something that hadn't happened in ages. I controlled this beast I'd become, not the other way around.

"You can stay here with me until the storm's over," I grumbled.

There was no way I'd let my wi—

No!

She wasn't my wife. Not truly. I hadn't sought marriage to her, and I would end this farce as quickly as possible.

But I couldn't let Nettie (that was a better way to refer to her, not *wife*) try to make it to town by herself in a raging storm.

Chapter 3
Nettie

"Thank you," I said carefully, studying Ryett. He looked the same as in his picture, from his horns to his thumb claws to his glorious wings tucked against his spine. Even the same guarded look shone in his pretty dark eyes.

I struggled not to give into dismay. How had I jumped from one tenuous situation into the next?

I slid off the chair he'd placed me in as if I was a two-year-old who'd nearly rushed out in a storm willy-nilly.

"Take your coat off," he said, rounding the island as if he needed a barrier between us. "Take everything off, actually. I'll toss your clothing into the dryer." His gaze shot to my bag. "I assume you've got other things you can wear in there?"

I nodded. I should feel like crying, right? Instead, I couldn't stop peeking at my new husband through my lashes. He hadn't greeted me with flowers, a smile, or a nice dinner, but I still found him very appealing. Maybe it was his hawkish nose. Or his gorgeous wings I wanted to stroke.

Or the loneliness I still found in his eyes.

He stepped over to my bag and hefted it, smacking it over his shoulder, and left the open kitchen connecting to a big living room with squishy appearing furniture and a woodstove sitting in front of a stone fireplace. "Come with me. I'll show you where you can change."

I followed him through the two-story room with a wall of glass overlooking the valley, and then we walked down a hall. Rain pelted the front windows, and whistling wind echoed through the house. We passed a bathroom on the right and ended up in a large bedroom.

Shaking my head, I gnashed my teeth. I couldn't believe I'd fallen for his mother's ruse. How could a woman do that to her son, let alone a woman she'd never met?

"You can change in here," Ryett said, dropping my bag on the floor beside a huge bed and backing toward the open doorway. His hand hooked onto the handle. "Bring your wet things out when you're done."

He shut the door, and his footsteps retreated down the hall.

I lifted my bag and dropped it onto the big bed, taking in the homemade patchwork quilt, an old mahogany bureau standing on one wall, and an oversized rocking chair sitting near a double window. A smaller, diamond-shaped window had been mounted in the wall above the bed to let in moonlight. Rain pelted the glass surface, slithering down it like big tears.

I sniffed, but I would not allow myself to cry. This hadn't turned out how I'd expected, but that didn't mean it was over yet. For now, I was his wife. And while I'd corresponded with his mother (ugh), bits of Ryett had come through. That was the guy I'd half fallen for.

Would it be worth seeing if we could create something from this? He didn't appear too interested in the idea, but he'd just met me.

With the storm raging outside, we had time to get to know each other. If he still wanted to end it after the storm had passed, I wouldn't fight him. What I'd do once he jilted me, I couldn't say. Maybe there was a place for me in the small town I'd passed through to get here. I could settle in, find a job, and build a new life.

I unzipped my bag and groaned when I found everything wet.

Peering around, I spied a t-shirt lying across the back of the rocking chair. Picking it up, I sniffed it, though I wasn't sure why. It smelled like . . . the forest on a sunny day. A man. And it contained the same hint of sadness I'd found in Ryett.

I poked around in the bureau but didn't find anything I dared touch. My hips were broad, though he was much bigger overall than me. Holding his shirt against my body showed it would hang to my mid-thighs. It pretty much resembled a nightshirt.

Would he mind if I borrowed it?

I didn't have much choice. I couldn't pull off wet clothing and dress in equally saturated things.

Even my bra and panties were wet. I hauled everything off and laid them across my bag.

I was tugging his shirt over my head when his bedroom door opened.

Ryett poked his head inside. "Would you like—" His gaze traveled down my half-naked frame. "I'm sorry. I, um, *did* knock."

I hadn't heard him.

He gulped as I yanked his shirt down over my hips.

Chapter 4
Ryett

Damn, her curves were tempting.

I smacked my palm over my eyes, but it was too late. I'd seen more than I should.

And I craved what she had to offer.

"I'm sorry," I growled, irritated at myself for opening the door without waiting for her to call out. "I didn't mean to barge in."

I was still angry with my mother for putting me in this position, though it was clear Nettie was as innocent in this farce of a marriage as me.

I'd barely reached the kitchen before storming back down the hall to ask her if she was hungry. Thirsty. If she needed . . . *anything*.

I didn't like that I couldn't stay away from her, that I ached to remain within her orbit.

And now I'd let the wyvern out of the cave, so to speak. My cock was charging against my pants, insisting I needed to woo her, seduce her if possible, and make this marriage real.

No!

I would not be coerced into doing something I hadn't stepped into on my own. Besides, Nettie couldn't have known she was being married by proxy to a monster. Once she realized that, she'd scurry from my house as fast as she could. I'd never hear from her again other than papers arriving in the mail needing a signature to end this before it got started.

"No true harm done," she said, one side of her lush mouth curving up. Her gorgeous eyes sparkled.

Damn me for noticing things like that.

"I pulled the shirt down fast," she added. "I doubt you saw much."

I'd seen *so* much. I wanted to see more.

"That's my shirt." It looked amazing on her, as if she'd wrapped herself in me.

"Yes," she said calmly. "All my things are wet. I hope you don't mind me wearing it. I can't exactly walk about naked."

Oh, hell, yeah, she could.

No, she shouldn't.

Why was my mind arguing with me?

I growled.

Her eyebrows lifted. "I'll take it off if you're that proprietary about your things." Her hands reached for the hem.

"No." I huffed and pivoted to keep her from seeing my stiff cock ramming itself against the front of my pants.

"You can wear it until your things are dry." I pivoted back and studiously ignoring her, snatched her bag off my bed. I stomped to the bathroom and wrenched open the cabinet doors to shove her things into the dryer. Closing the hatch, I started it.

I turned and bumped into Nettie, grasping her upper arms to keep us both from falling sideways. The misstep brought us close together. Her right boob compressed against my left arm, and I swore her nipple hardened.

My cock knocked on my pants again, eager to get out. Damn thing.

"Why did you follow me?" I asked.

Her low chuckle rang out, and the husky sound wasn't helping me suppress my unruly cock. "I wanted to help."

"You don't need to help." I lifted her and finding there wasn't enough room to place her where she'd be out of the way, I looped my arms under her ripe ass and around her back and, turning sideways, carried her out into the hall and down to the kitchen.

I did not notice how amazing she smelled.

I did not notice how she wrapped her arms around my shoulders and snuggled against my chest as if she wasn't repulsed by being held by a wyvern.

And I didn't have the overwhelming urge to kiss her.

Chapter 5
Nettie

Outside, the storm continued, wind gusting against the building and whistling eerily, as if ghosts had surrounded the house and were trying to batter their way through.

He seemed to want to carry me around everywhere, and since it felt good to be held by him, I didn't protest too much.

"You should put me down," I said. "I can walk."

He paused in the kitchen and looked down at me, his gaze focused on my mouth. If I didn't know better, I'd think he wanted to kiss me. But that couldn't be. Nope, he wanted to divorce me.

I'd rather have a kiss. Would it be wrong to pursue him, to try to salvage something from this marriage? I couldn't seem to stop myself from trying.

He lowered me to my feet in the kitchen and backed away, his hands lifting. "I didn't mean to do that."

"It's okay," I said with a shrug. "I don't mind you carrying me."

"You don't?" His scowl took over his confused expression. "I'm a wyvern. I was turned into this beastly thing when I drank that infernal brew."

"I've read about Dr. Karloff and how he turned a bunch of the Screaming Woods residents into monsters. Whatever happened to him?"

He shrugged. "I don't know, and I don't care. The damage was already done. Seeking retribution wouldn't turn me back into a human. I've learned to live with it."

"Moving forward's a good thing." I tiptoed around him, aiming for the living room.

"I can't imagine what I'd do if something like that happened to me," I said, peeking over my shoulder at him, though he was turned away. "I imagine you were scared at first. Angry."

"Both."

When he didn't look at me, I studied his glorious, leathery folded wings that spiked up over his shoulders. The tips hung down below his knees.

"I had to accept it, since there was no going back." He cleared his throat and peered at me over his shoulder, his gaze locking onto my face. Did he think he'd see revulsion there?

"Your wings are amazing."

Pivoting to face me, he snorted. "I agree—now. At first? The damn things got in the way all the time. I couldn't go through a room without knocking stuff over or off shelves. And they used to hurt when I laid on them.

Now, they're not so bad. I've figured out how to keep them flat on my back. It's fun to fly."

"I can't imagine." I shot him a grin. "Maybe someday you could . . ." No, it would be wrong to ask him for anything like that.

"Maybe I could what, Nettie?" He watched me intently, and I sensed my answer mattered.

I shrugged. "I think it would be wonderful to fly too."

"I'd have to hold you." A vein throbbed in his temple, and a bit of smoke coiled from his nostrils. It should be repulsive, but instead, it made sparks fly through me, heating me up faster than something this simple should.

"Maybe I'd like that." Unable to stay away, I took a step closer to him.

"How could you enjoy anything like that?"

"I knew you were a wyvern when I agreed to marry you. I have a picture." One I wouldn't share since it was obvious I'd touched it, *stroked* it a billion times. "To me, you're the whole package."

Frowning, he grunted. "You didn't gasp and cringe when you saw this for the first time?" He gestured to his body.

"Why should I? It's what's inside someone that counts, not wings or claws," I boldly flicked one of the two-inch claws on his thumbs, "or horns." I jumped up to tap one, but he was too tall for me to reach. Instead, my fingers slid down his shoulder, and I noted the ripped muscles beneath his shirt. "All of this is you, and I find you appealing."

"You can't." He backed away and rounded the island. "No one can."

"You're wrong, Ryett. *I* find you very attractive."

Chapter 6
Ryett

I blinked at her for a moment, stunned. "You had my picture. My freakin' mom wrote you emails. Please tell me you didn't fall in love with some fantasy you created about me."

Her chin trembled, but she held it up. "I see you for who you are now."

A grumpy, bitter guy, most likely.

No, that wasn't completely true. She'd just said she found me attractive.

I'd never thought I'd experience love with a woman or marry. Who'd want to be with a wyvern other than someone looking for a sick thrill? Not long after I was changed, I'd seen women come to town just to meet monsters. The titillation factor excited them. One of them even found a way into my home and climbed into my bed.

I'd kicked her out, of course. If I was with someone, I

wanted it to be real. There wasn't anything wrong with needing something like that.

And now Nettie seemed to be offering it. Did I dare take a chance?

I couldn't imagine why I was even thinking this. The snarl working its way up from inside me barked into the air.

I had to hand it to Nettie. She didn't even flinch. Instead, her breath caught, and the scent of something I couldn't define hung in the air. It made my cock twitch, inappropriate thing that it was.

"Are you hungry?" I asked. "I can make you something."

"Sure." Her face softened. "Can I help?" She strode past me, into the kitchen.

I didn't notice how my shirt hugged her curves or how it swayed enticingly across the tops of her thighs.

Damn she looked good in my clothing. With her tousled hair, I could imagine her fresh from my bed after we'd been together. She'd only tugged my shirt on because she wanted to feel something of mine wrapped around her.

She smelled like new rain, happiness, and hope, along with a hint of . . . nah, it couldn't be arousal. She might've been willing to marry me, but I bet she would've laid in the bed our first night like a statue while I grunted over her.

It was natural to fear rejection. I'd lived with this form for years, and I'd seen too many people shrink away when they saw me walking down the street.

And many slunk from town, never to reach out to us again—like my dad.

"I don't need help," I said, following her. "I can do it."

"I like to cook. You do one part, and I'll do another." She stepped toward the fridge.

I grabbed her arm to hold her back. "No."

She didn't cringe at my touch, and terror didn't fill her eyes. In fact, they went limpid, like I truly *had* just loved her body completely and she wanted me to do it again.

Whatever she was thinking, it wasn't about shrugging away. She leaned closer, her head tipping back as if she wanted my kiss . . .

Releasing her, I shook my head and put a few steps between us. Perhaps I feared rejection more than I should. But few other than my mother saw the real me instead of the wyvern beast who'd consumed my exterior.

Could Nettie? For one second, I softened. I leaned toward her; my gaze locked on her mouth.

She sucked in a breath and stepped so close, the tips of her hard nipples brushed my chest.

"Go sit in the living room," I barked, reeling backward, irritated that her being close could ignite this much longing inside me. "Don't come near me."

Her laughter trilled out, something I had not expected. I thought she'd wince or that tears would spring up in her eyes.

"Why? Are you afraid I might *touch* you?" She poked my arm, making my scaly skin quiver. "Or that you might find you enjoy doing something with me?"

I would, and that was the problem.

"I don't bite, though I might be persuaded to nibble," she said gaily. "Do you need some nibbling, Ryett?" Pivoting away from me, she opened the fridge and leaned forward, removing vegetables out of the crisper drawer. "I'll make a salad."

My damn shirt rode up. I couldn't see everything, but I didn't need to. I could imagine it perfectly well.

She was too enticing, too much fun to be around, and too determined to show me she wasn't frightened by my gruffness or appearance.

Was I stupid not to open my heart enough to see if she was willing to step inside?

When her butt wiggled, and my shirt shimmied up to the crest of her ass, I couldn't resist. I took her arm and tugged her around, pressing her back against the counter beside the fridge. The lettuce she held crunched between us.

"Ryett," she breathed, looking up at me.

Fuck me, but I couldn't hold myself back any longer. I just needed one taste, then I could set her aside and get on with my life.

I lifted her up and kissed her.

Chapter 7
Nettie

All my dreams were coming true, and I found them in Ryett's arms.

His mouth slanted across mine, and I wrapped my legs and arms around him, clinging, grinding against him.

He tasted wonderful, like something untamed.

I opened my mouth, and his tongue slid across mine.

We both groaned.

He flung one arm out, sending the veggies I'd placed on the counter flying, then settled my butt on the surface, pressing against the back of my ass with his big palm to bring me to the edge. His long, spiked tail whipped around my waist, keeping me from falling.

While the storm raged outside, a cyclone hit the interior, one composed of us. I whimpered and tugged at his clothing as he deftly slid his fingers up between my thighs, spreading me for his touch.

When he stroked the pad of his thumb between my legs, his head reeled back, and he hissed. "You're wet."

Yeah, because it felt good. There was something about Ryett that completely turned me on.

I leaned back, urging my body closer to his, spreading my thighs wider.

He watched my face as he slid one finger inside me.

"Too wet," he growled, pushing another finger in to join the first. His thumb claw glided across my clit.

My moan ripped from me, bringing the hint of a smile to his mouth. He was hot even without humor in his eyes and a devilish smile on his lips. When he grinned, he was so devastating, I swooned.

With his gaze locked on mine, he pumped his fingers in and out, his claw tracing across my clit that craved whatever he had to offer.

I might not have a ton of experience with guys. It had been too hard to sneak out of my father's place.

But I knew my body. It was having the time of its life.

His fingers went faster. His claw pressed down harder.

I ground myself into his touch, my cries echoing around us.

Wiggling and squealing, I clung to his shoulders, watching his face crater with lust as my body shot toward complete satisfaction. I wanted him to rip off his pants and drive himself inside me, something I'd never craved from a guy before.

His fingers moved faster. His claw left my clit, only to be replaced with his other hand.

When he rolled my clit, I shrieked, giving way like an avalanche roaring down a hillside. Nothing and no one was going to stop me from drawing every scrap of pleasure I could from Ryett's touch.

I shuddered, rocking on the counter as one orgasm after another bolted through me.

Collapsing against him, I grinned into his shirt.

Maybe this was the start of something between me and Ryett, something real and true and lasting. Something we could turn into a real marriage.

His fingers slowed, and his hand went around me to support me as I sucked in the last bit of pleasure he delivered.

I kissed his chest, though I doubted he'd feel the gesture through his shirt.

He might think there was nothing between us, but I was going to prove him wrong.

By the time this storm was over, he would tell me he'd changed his mind, that he didn't want to send me away.

Chapter 8
Ryett

Now she'd do it.

She'd shove me away and demand I never touch her again. She'd shriek that she hated me for taking advantage of the moment. She'd insist she wanted me to stay away from her until she could flee my home and file for divorce.

Instead, she pressed her forehead into my shirt. "That was amazing." Leaning back, she looked up at me, grinning. "Can we do it again?" Her frown took in my stiff cock pressing against the front of my pants, and she reached out to stroke it through the fabric, making it surge into her touch. "Poor you. You're still like a rock." She started unfastening my pants. "Let me—"

"No!" I unwrapped myself from around her and backed away, my hands lifting. Her musky scent clung to my fingers, and I wanted to lick every drop of her off them.

Shit, I was in deep trouble.

"I suppose you're right," she said with a happy sigh, hopping off the counter and tugging my adopted shirt back down around her thighs. "I only arrived today. While I assumed we'd get to things like this eventually, you said—actually *your mom*—said you'd give me time to get to know you before we jumped into the sack together." She peeked up at me through her lashes. "Do you feel like you know me enough yet to do something like that?"

Imp.

My heart roared.

I couldn't speak; I could only sputter with the irritation I struggled to maintain. Despite my aching cock, I wanted to smile along with her. Chuckle and take her hand. I'd lead her down the hall, strip off my shirt and kiss every inch of her skin. I'd lay her on the bed and climb all over her. We wouldn't emerge from my bedroom for weeks.

"It doesn't seem fair," she sighed.

"What doesn't?" Instead of daydreaming, why wasn't I running away from her? I could lock myself in the unfinished basement. Or the barn. She could have the run of the house until the storm ended. Then she'd leave. I'd never need to see her again, dream about what she could give me again.

Instead, I hung around her like a sappy teenager with his first crush, clinging to her every word.

"It's not fair that I had so much fun while you didn't." She reached toward me again. "Are you sure I can't take care of your little problem? I could . . . take a taste and see what happens after that."

Damn she had a trashy mouth.

I loved it.

"Don't come near me," I snarled.

"Yeah, that's what you said a short time ago. I'm glad you changed your mind."

"I did not change my mind," I snapped, feeling completely out of control of her and this situation. "We will not be having sex."

"Probably not tonight, though if you were interested, I have a feeling I could be persuaded." Lifting the lettuce off the floor, she scowled at it. "Good thing it's still inside the package. I always wash it anyway, don't you?" Ripping into it, she held it under the faucet, spraying it. "I try to buy organic when I can. I figure I don't need to eat pesticides in everything, and what's a few bugs in comparison to something like that? Protein, I always say. As long as I don't see them, I can pretend they're not there."

"You chatter too much."

She shot me a grin over her shoulder. "Then get busy, and you can focus on something other than me. I saw some chicken in the fridge. Do you have a grill? I love barbecued chicken." She started opening the cupboards, eventually huffing. "No barbecue sauce. How do you survive?"

"I char my meat."

"Oh." Her mouth formed a circle. "You mean you use your dragon flames to cook it?"

"*Wyvern*, not dragon. There's a big difference."

"I did look it up online." Her head tilted. "Wyverns are not full dragons, though they have many of the parts." Her gaze zoned in on my groin. "Are you a dragon down there?"

"I'm not going to tell you," I bellowed.

"Sorry. That was impertinent of me. I'll try to keep away from personal questions." Wiggling her lush body, she ran her fingers across her lips as if she zipped them closed.

If only it was truly possible to keep her from speaking. Like a steamroller, she was roaring across me, pressing me flat on the ground like a rug. I imagined her stepping all over me after that while I gazed up at her in adoration.

No!

Not adoration. *Irritation.* That was all I'd ever feel for her.

"*Can* you barbecue food with your flames?" she asked as she rinsed cucumbers.

"If I wish."

She clapped her hands. "Can I watch?"

My cock surged as if she'd suggested she watch me jerk off.

"Watch you cook the food, silly." She tapped my arm before turning back to the counter. "Good thing I enjoy a dirty mind. It melds well with mine."

My ears went hot. Flames broiled inside me, and it was all I could do not to stomp out onto my deck and let them blaze into the sky.

"Is there anything else you'd like with your chicken and salad?" she asked as she tore lettuce and tossed it into a big bowl. "I could make some smashed potatoes if you have any around."

"I don't want potatoes," I grumbled.

"Are you doing low carb?" she asked as she started chopping carrots. "I sometimes do it myself; it's a great way to lose weight."

"I'm not doing low carb."

"Yeah, I cheat a lot too. I saw some ice cream in your freezer. We can have that for dessert."

Whatever control I tried to grasp onto slipped through my fingers, tugged away by this infernal female. "It's *my* ice cream."

"You can share it. Maybe we'll eat out of the same bowl. I can feed you, and you can feed me. Or we could dig into the carton and skip the bowl. I'm okay with that too."

Perhaps a hasty retreat was in order. I could regroup and be ready to lead the next charge in this battle with my wife.

No!

She was only a *temporary* wife. I'd divorce her as soon as I could. She'd leave, and my tidy world would return to the way it was before.

Quieter and lonelier, but that was the way I wanted it to be.

Not really, but—

"It's the way I want it," I huffed.

"Good. I love cookies and cream, and your container

looks half full. In no time, you're going to see that we can have a lot of fun together."

I was afraid she was right.

With a wince, I pivoted and strode from the kitchen. A retreat was definitely in order. "I'll go start the grill."

Chapter 9
Nettie

I was behaving hella cheeky, but I couldn't seem to hold it back. Ryett was so cute and grumbly, which was my favorite romance trope. How could I resist sliding into the sunshine role?

Besides, there was something highly stimulating about his snaps and snarls. If he knew, he'd stop doing it—or try to—so I wasn't going to tell him.

I really didn't want to force him into anything. What we did on the counter probably shouldn't happen again. He'd made it clear he didn't want me, and I needed to accept that.

Why couldn't I?

Maybe because his damn eyes reflected sadness when he might not realize I was looking. I recognized the feeling, and it kept sucking me in.

After dinner, we sat in the living room, him on the couch, me in a stiff, upright chair.

Rain beat on the roof, a steady drum. When the wind

hit the building in just the right way, it howled, trying to find a way inside. But it was cozy inside his log cabin. There wasn't any place I'd rather be.

"Stormy," I said.

"Which is why you're here."

Yeah, keep reminding me.

His TV wasn't working due to the weather, so I stared at my hands and fidgeted my feet on the hardwood floor. I'd look around for books tomorrow to occupy my mind. Otherwise, I'd spew endless chatter and drive Ryett out of his mind.

"Dessert?" I asked.

He stared at his bare feet that had cute little claws on his toes, saying nothing. Nothing was basically agreement, right?

Rather than get a bowl, I grabbed the ice cream container from the freezer and a spoon. I dropped onto the couch beside him, and if our thighs happened to rub together, that was okay. I needed to be close if I was going to share the treat.

I scooped up a bite and dangled it in front of his mouth.

He glared at it.

"Open up. You don't need a choo-choo do you?"

"What?" His gaze met mine.

Yup, I still saw the guy I'd married in there; he just needed to find a way out. Maybe I was wrong to keep hoping my dreams of Ryett came true.

I'd certainly speak my mind to his mother if and when she showed up. But I sensed she spoke to me from *his* heart in her emails. It was clear she knew Ryett well. She'd picked me, and how was that any different from matchmakers of old? If this was the wild west, and I was a mail-order bride, he wouldn't know me any better than he did now.

"Choo-choo? What are you talking about?" he asked in a fairly normal tone. Maybe his grumpiness was sliding off his scaly hide—a sad thing right there.

"A train, like they do with little kids." I lifted my voice. "Here comes a bite on the choo-choo. Open wide and let the engine into the tunnel."

He shook his head and sighed, but he opened his mouth.

Progress.

While he swirled the ice cream around in his mouth and swallowed, I took my own bite, wiggling at how yummy it was.

"I try not to keep stuff like this around," I said as I gathered up more for him on the spoon. "Cookies and cake, too. My weight isn't where I'd like it to be, but—"

"You look fine the way you are."

I tilted my head back to look at his face and for once, I didn't find frustrated irritation there. Definite progress. "Do you think so? Many women are skinnier than me."

"You're lush. Curvy. I like that in a woman."

"Well, that's good then."

I fed him more ice cream, and he didn't balk at each bite, alternating with feeding myself. After we'd polished off what was left in the container, I dumped it in the trash and returned to the living room, dropping back down on the sofa beside him.

He shifted away from me.

I inched closer.

He moved again.

I did the same.

"You're going to fall off if you perch on the arm," I pointed out.

"Why do you want to be close to me?"

"Because I like you." I was being completely honest. Despite his gruff demeanor, I found him cute and charming.

"You can't. You shouldn't."

"Because you intend to throw me away once the storm is through?"

"A woman like you would never want to be with a wyvern."

"And yet, here I am, trying to sit close to a wyvern to show you that I like you, and I'm quite happy being married to you."

"It won't last," he said. "It never does."

"What do you mean by that?"

"Women don't want to be with monsters. That's all I'm saying."

I snarled. "Who did this to you?"

"Did what?"

"I assume you're saying a woman rejected you." I'd rip her head off.

"She was right to tell me we were through."

My heart pinched at the hollow sound of his voice.

"She was wrong." My words came out soft, gentle. "She doesn't know what she's missing."

"I imagine she does. She's married to someone else and has three kids now."

"I want kids, do you?" I asked, though kindly.

"I always wanted kids, but there's no chance of that now."

"Are you sterile?"

"How the hell would I know?"

I shrugged. "Sperm testing?"

"I haven't had that," he huffed. "I meant kids aren't part of my future. What if they're born with wings?"

"Then you could give them flying lessons."

"It can't happen."

It could if he'd give me a chance. I sensed I could love him. It was silly on my part, perhaps, because it seemed I was doomed to have my heart crushed beneath his foot. I couldn't seem to help it. I was drawn to him like no one else, and I wasn't so silly that I wouldn't try to grab onto what felt like the best thing in my life.

I moved closer to him.

He leapt off the end of the sofa. "Let's go to bed."

Standing, I crinkled my eyes at him. "Sex so soon? I thought we were going to take time to get to know each other first?"

Chapter 10
Ryett

Unable to do more than sputter—again—I stomped from the living room and down the hall. It was only when I reached the end and my bedroom that I could admit defeat. I'd run away.

She was amazing. No wonder my mom "picked" her out for me. I was upset about that. Who wouldn't be? But I also wasn't stupid.

Nettie believed we were married, and it appeared she wasn't going to back down.

She was fighting for me, something only my mom had done before. Everyone else turned their back on me, fled rather than look me in the eye. I hadn't wanted sympathy when I was changed. I was too damn bullheaded—or *wyvern*-headed—for that. I'd only wanted a touch of understanding.

No, I'd wanted acceptance. If everyone could treat me like I was the same person—which I was!—then I could do it as well.

Retreating from Nettie was a wise move on my part. I needed to regroup and figure out how to handle this.

I was much too attracted to her. I could barely be in the same room with her without wanting to kiss her. Touch her. *Please* her.

What should I do about it?

I knew what my body wanted to do, but I still felt coerced into this, though I no longer blamed Nettie. She was as innocent in this as me. If anything, she had more reason to feel angry.

I still couldn't believe my mom not only found Nettie but also conversed with her for months. She'd made Nettie like me, and that was totally wrong. I mean, I was a likeable enough guy—sometimes. But my mom had taken advantage of a person with a good heart.

I needed to reject her.

Or did I? Maybe it wouldn't be so bad to be nice to her, to get to know her. We had days before the storm was over. Once it ended, I could come to a final decision.

Wait, wait, wait.

What the hell was I thinking? I didn't want a wife. I didn't want Nettie.

Not too much, that is.

It didn't matter at the moment. I had another, even bigger problem, if there was such a thing in this rat's nest of a situation.

My cabin had one bedroom. One bed.

Nettie trotted into the bedroom, still chattering. "I didn't bring protection. I guess I felt if we did it, you might have some."

I snorted but didn't dare turn her way.

"They don't make condoms that fit wyverns," I growled, feeling proud for maintaining my irritated manner. It was part of my wall, of course, raised to protect me from having my heart broken all over again. I was savvy enough to see it, though I wouldn't let on to Nettie.

"Now isn't that intriguing?" she said, joining me in my bedroom. "Condoms don't fit? You're either incredibly small or—"

I snarled.

She flashed me a grin. "Caught you. You know you don't need to be this grumpy all the time. It might do you good to lighten up every now and then."

Saying nothing, I lifted one eyebrow her way.

"You do know I'm teasing. I like you, but I'm going to be honest here. I'm not sure it would be wise for us to have sex right away."

Rejection now that I'd almost convinced myself to give this a chance? "Why not?" I huffed.

"Because then we can't get an annulment."

"What if I don't want one?" There, I'd thrown it out at her, hinted at my feelings.

"I believe we both have to agree on something like that."

Talk about confusing me. "Are you saying you do, or you don't want an annulment?"

She reached up to stroke her fingertip along my jaw. "Let's see what happens over the next few days, shall we?"

While she hadn't exactly thrown herself at me, she'd shown she was interested. She also told me she was, though I still wasn't sure why.

Now she was backing away?

Women. They were too complicated for my peace of mind. I'd be wise to reject her like everyone else.

"Yes, we shall see," was all I was willing to offer.

She gave me a pert nod. "I guess I should check out my clothing in the dryer and find something to wear to bed." Her eyes widened, and she smacked her palm against her mouth.

"What's the problem?" I asked.

"Please realize I thought I was coming here to meet a guy I'd half fallen in love with, one I was willing to fall the rest of the way in love with once I got to know him better."

Did this mean she *didn't* want an annulment?

And people said guys had difficulty communicating.

"I went shopping," she said. "You—your mom—sent a bit of money for a trousseau."

I wasn't even sure what a trousseau was, but I nodded, encouraging her to continue.

"I bought a few things." She held up her hand when I took a step away from her. "I understand! I can wear this." She tugged on my shirt that looked damn good on her. Better than any fancy gown or something barely there . . .

My mind dove into the idea, picturing Nettie's lush body dressed only in a slinky, high-cut nightie. Or a thong.

My cock roared to life.
Fuck, I was in deep trouble.

Chapter 11
Nettie

"I don't mind wearing your shirt," I said. Actually, I loved wearing it. It smelled like a promise. The fire we'd lit in the kitchen.

Him.

"But I could put on something else instead," I said. "For all I know, you only have a few shirts, and you need this one."

"You can wear whatever you want." He backed toward the door. "I'll sleep in the living room."

I frowned, unsure why he'd choose to squish his big frame onto the sofa. "Why?"

"Because this is the only bed."

"Oh, I see." Heat rose in my face. One bed was almost a cliché, though I enjoyed that trope as much as grumpy sunshine. "I can take the sofa."

"You won't."

"Now you're behaving like a gentleman, Ryett?" I teased. "I don't mind the sofa."

"I will take it," he growled.

"Such a temper." I tapped his chest because I couldn't seem to stop from making a physical connection between us. What we'd done in the kitchen kept haunting me. He growled and grumbled, but the guy who'd given me that much pleasure wasn't completely indifferent to me. It gave me hope that we could salvage something from this marriage.

"I have a reason to be grumpy," he said.

"I suppose you do. I can't imagine drinking something that was supposed to be fun, only to wake up completely changed."

He grunted.

"As for the bed," I studied it, "king sized, I believe. We can share. There's no reason for either of us to be uncomfortable."

"I'm not going to sleep with you."

"And I'd never ask you to do anything more than sleep." Would a good night's rest make him more approachable? Although, I very much enjoyed his snarling demeanor. It sparked all kinds of interesting feelings inside me.

He wasn't the guy I'd corresponded with. He wasn't the guy I'd married by proxy.

But I sensed I could love this guy even more than the fake one I'd built a lifetime of dreams around.

This one generated incredible lust inside me, something I couldn't say about anyone else.

"You'd lay in a bed with me?" he asked, his head tilting.

"We both need to sleep. There's no reason not to be practical about this. You're not going to attack me in the night."

"I may look like a monster, but it doesn't go past my exterior."

"You're sweet inside. I just know it."

His scowl deepened.

"Let me grab my things from the dryer then, and I'll scoot into the bathroom to change." As much as it would kill me to take off his shirt, I had my own things I could now wear. "If it's okay, I'll take the bathroom first. Then you can change into your PJs after me. I'll turn off the light and get under the covers. You won't even know I'm there."

"I don't have PJs."

"You sleep au naturel, then?"

"I have a tail. It's hard to find clothing that accommodates something like that, though I discovered a place online recently."

"I guess you could wear your underwear, then," I said pertly. I paused in the doorway, looking back at him. He stared at the bed while raking both of his hands through his hair and across his horns.

What would it be like to touch those horns, to grip them tightly while he . . . I really needed to stop thinking about sex.

"I promise to stay on my side of the bed," I said. "I won't encroach, and I won't attack you either."

Though I'd be sorely tempted. Consent was a good thing, however, and despite our wild moment in the kitchen, we needed to back things off until we got to know each other better.

He said nothing, just watched me.

With a nod, I left the room, taking the hallway to the bathroom, where I found the washer and dryer behind a set of doors. I brushed my teeth. Opting to take a shower, I dressed in what I'd brought so optimistically for our first night together.

What would he think of my nightie? I'd tried to pick something that was cute but a little bit sexy. When I tried it on, it gave me a boost of confidence, something a girl needed for her first night in her marriage bed.

Actually, I should be hoping the light was out when I returned to the room, that he'd opted to do his teeth—fangs—in the kitchen and get under the covers. He'd be snoring away, and I could slide under the blankets and remain on my side of the bed. Neither of us would know the other was there.

And who was I kidding? I could feel his presence in the bathroom with the door shut. He was a category ten hurricane roaring toward shore, assuming there were hurricanes that strong. They could call this one Ryett.

I left the bathroom and stepped into the dark hall. The wind continued to howl outside, and rain pelted the roof, a dull roar. Should I be worried about flooding or a landslide? Ryett didn't seem concerned, so I would hold off thinking about it until morning.

He'd turned all the lights off.

I crept down the hall, pausing in his open doorway.

A bang rang out behind me, coming from the kitchen, where a dim light still shone.

"Ryett?" I whispered, unsure why I didn't speak in a normal voice. Maybe the darkness had swallowed the courage I'd drummed up inside the bathroom. Or maybe the haunting wind and endless rain made me jittery.

When I didn't hear anything, I tiptoed down the hall to the kitchen, pausing before stepping out into the light.

Ahead of me, he swore, though softly.

I inched forward, moving across the living room, around the island, and up to where he had dropped to his hands and knees on the floor and stuffed his head beneath the kitchen sink.

Crouching, I tapped him on the shoulder.

He jerked upward, smacking his head on the underpart of the sink. His roar echoed from the small space, and his tail snapped out, coiling around my waist.

He backed from beneath the sink fast and flung himself on top of me, taking me down to the floor, though I didn't hit hard.

Looming over me, he snarled. "What the—" His eyes widened, and his voice softened. "Nettie."

"Yes, I . . . I'm sorry, I . . ." I couldn't seem to focus on anything but the wild hair he'd released from the band that now half covered his face, the fact that he wore nothing but boxers, plus the lust growing in his eyes as they slid to my chest.

"What are you wearing?" he asked.

"My nightgown." I swallowed, but my burgeoning desire would not go down. "I mentioned it."

"Nettie," he growled, his eyes locked on the swell of my breasts above the black nightie. "That is not a night-gown. It's a . . . shit."

"It's not shit," I said with a low chuckle. "I'll have you know I purchased this especially for you. Or for . . ." I wasn't bringing his mom into this heady moment.

"For *me*," he said softly. "You bought it to wear for me."

"I just said that."

"You bought it for me to peel off you, I think."

An aching need shot through my body, centering in my core. My clit tightened.

"Would you like me to peel it off you now, Nettie?" he asked.

Chapter 12
Ryett

What's a guy need to do to find time to fix a drip under the sink?

The drip was essentially forgotten, swept away by this luscious, desirable woman.

She bought this "nightgown," *for me*, a slip of silk with a few specks of lace and only a thread sliding between her legs.

"Tell me to back off and leave you alone," I said, near the end of my line. I teetered on the edge. One nudge on her part, and I'd tumble down the other side.

"I don't think I can," she whispered.

Heaven help me, but I couldn't resist her. But she'd only arrived here today. So while I'd almost kill to drive my cock inside her, I would not do it.

I lifted her off her feet and swept down the hall, laying her carefully on my bed.

With a growl, I climbed over her and captured her mouth, savoring how she tasted and the tiny moans she released from this simple touch. I'd finger fucked her in my kitchen, and now I was going to suck on her clit until she exploded again.

Then I would back off and leave her alone. I'd lie next to her, though it was doubtful I'd sleep, and keep my hands to myself.

Leaving her mouth, I kissed down her neck and across her upper chest, pausing at the mounds of her breasts peeking above the black satin.

She clung to my horns, and hell, that felt amazing. When she stroked them, shockwaves shot from them to my cock, making it ache with need. Holding myself back was going to be tough, but I'd find a way.

Smoke coiled from my nostrils, but I waved my hand, dissipating it.

I snagged the lace at the top of her nightie with my fangs and tugged it down. One ripe breast burst free. The nipple had formed a hard bud—also for me. Everything about this female was perfect, from her ripe shape to her sharp wit. She made me think and feel in a way I never had before.

While she stroked my horns, I sucked her nipple into my mouth, stretching back a bit to tug. It took next to no time to expose the other, and my fingers got to work, rolling it while I nibbled on the first with my fangs. I'd never bitten anyone, but a primal need to do so kept cresting inside me. Would Nettie let me do something like that? Not hard, just enough to mark her.

All I could picture was riding her from behind while I gave her that mark on her shoulder.

Mine, everything inside me cried.

Was this my inner beast speaking? How would I know? The change burst through me when I was fifteen after drinking that brew. Back then, I was a skinny nerdy guy with next to no muscles and only a thin spark of interest in girls. I hadn't kissed anyone, and I sure as hell hadn't pumped my fingers inside anyone.

Sure, I'd been with women since. They flocked to me by the time I was eighteen because I was big, full of attitude, and I had wings. The titillation factor kept them coming, and I took what they offered, smartening up within a year when I started feeling used.

I'd been with no one since.

Keeping her sweet nipple in my mouth, I slid my palm across her silk-clad belly and cupped her hip. She groaned and lifted herself toward me, her legs parting.

"Sweet," I said, leaving her nipple only long enough to see her face. Her eyes had closed, and her fingers writhed across my horns, stroking and tugging. My cock was on fire.

Easing down her body, I kissed across her belly and spread her legs wide.

"Yes," she said, her head jerking out a nod.

She smelled like hope and a future. Like love.

No!

Not love. I couldn't give my heart to her. But I could give her this.

Tugging the slice of fabric to the side, I licked her wet folds. Greed shot through me. She tasted amazing; I couldn't get enough. Finding her clit with my fingers, I stroked the ripe bud, grinning at how she twitched and moaned, pumping up to meet my touch.

I ran my fingertips through her folds, parting them until I could see her glistening passage. How in the world was I going to resist delving inside her with my cock? I'd have to be satisfied—for now—with giving her pleasure. Making her come a thousand times and more should do it.

When I drove my tongue inside her, she cried out, her voice echoing in the small room. Because she tasted so wonderful, I licked and sucked, eager to feel her explode.

Her clit almost throbbed, swelling with her heat. She writhed beneath me, arching up as her body climbed higher.

When she came, it was suddenly and with a big gush. I licked faster, determined that none of her satisfaction escaped my tongue. More shudders ripped through her, and her bliss tasted amazing.

She sagged on the bed, breathing fast, her fingers still swirling across my horns. "You're wrecking me."

Only once I was sure I'd sucked in each drop of her essence did I look up. "What do you mean?"

"How am I going to be with someone else after a performance like that?"

Chapter 13
Nettie

He didn't reply. Maybe he wasn't sure what to say. Or maybe he knew but felt now wasn't a good time to tell me—*again*—that he didn't want me.

He'd sure wanted me a second ago.

Patience, I told myself. We'd barely met. But despite only being with him for a short time, I felt like I'd known him forever. A cliché as much as the one bed and us being stranded together inside his cabin, but there it was.

He slid off the bed. Scooting around the foot, he climbed underneath the covers on his side.

Should I talk about what happened? I felt strangely vulnerable right now. Opening myself up to his snarls, as cute as I saw them, felt wrong for this moment. I needed to savor the memory of him sacrificing his own pleasure to make sure I found mine.

I eased to the side and pulled the covers up over my body.

With a grunt, he tugged me into his arms, rolled me onto my side, and spooned me. His upper arm wrapped tightly around me, his palm resting between my breasts.

I'd think about what all this meant in the morning.

For now, what we'd done was enough.

Chapter 14
Nettie

I woke to the ongoing drum of rain on the roof, intermittent gusts of wind, and a cool bed beside me. The amazing smell of something sweet cooking drifted through the air.

Stretching, I savored the hum deep within my bones that had settled in after he brought me to orgasm with his mouth. If I called out and he returned to the room, could I talk him into doing it again?

Somehow, I suspected he'd turn me down. Or growl, which wouldn't be all that unappealing.

Damn, I had it bad for him already.

Last night, my hope for something with Ryett had begun to waver, but who could feel discouraged after a guy licked her like that?

Now my merry mood had been restored. It was time to get up and share it with Ryett.

I dressed and tiptoed down the hall barefoot, stopping at the edge of the kitchen to watch him as he bustled about near the stove. He only wore low-slung pants, his tail projecting from a small slice in the back.

"Do you open the seam in the back of your pants then stitch around the hole so it won't unravel, or do you buy pants with holes incorporated into the back for your tail?" I asked.

Freezing in place with a spatula in his hand, he didn't turn to face me. "Monsters are mainstream now. Didn't you know? I order clothing that fits online."

"Then you could get PJs if you wanted to." I went over to the island, dragged out a high-back chair, and sat.

"Why would I need something like that?"

"To cover yourself at night?"

He snorted. "Would you like me to order PJs?"

Actually, no. "And miss out on the fun of seeing you strut around in skimpy boxers?" I said with a low laugh.

"My boxers aren't skimpy."

I suspected he wasn't quite ready to face me, but that was okay. This gave me a chance to drool over the play of muscles across his back as he moved around the small kitchen. And check out his glorious wings tucked against his spine.

"You're welcome to wear boxers around the house whenever you want." I smirked. "Since, as you say, they're not skimpy."

He paused at the stove, not turning, then continued cooking, flipping something in a pan that smelled wonderful.

"I'm making pancakes," he said.

"Yay. Love them. Chocolate chip?"

Turning, he frowned. "Who would put chocolate chips in pancakes?"

"Me. They taste good that way."

"I'm a pancake purist. I might consent to blueberries, but I'll never put chocolate chips in mine. I won't eat them either."

"I'll make them for you sometime. Then you can decide."

He grumbled.

I grinned. He was so much fun to tease.

"What's on the agenda today?" I asked. "Besides hanging out together. Do you want to do a puzzle or play some games?"

"I have things to do outside."

"Cool. I'll help."

His grunt rang out, though I wasn't sure if it indicated agreement or not.

He lifted a plate loaded with pancakes and strode over to the island to place it in the center. He collected dishes and silverware from the cabinets and syrup from the fridge, plunking them down on the island as well.

"This looks amazing." I sent him a shy smile. "Thank you for cooking breakfast. I'll make lunch or dinner or both."

He scratched the back of his neck. "Can you cook?"

"I made the salad last night, didn't I?"

With one eyebrow lifted, he served me half the stack of pancakes and took the rest for himself, sitting next to me. He slathered his pile of pancakes with butter and syrup. I did the same.

"What sort of food do you like?" I asked. He'd chowed through the salad last night, and his chicken had been grilled to perfection. "There are leftovers in the fridge. I could make a chicken salad." And a chocolate cake. Talking about chips had sparked my chocolate appetite, a voracious thing I made no attempt to hide.

"I guess that would be alright," he said pleasantly.

I was the one who'd had the orgasm, yet he'd softened as if I'd sucked him off, then rode him half the night.

Was he changing his mind about me?

"These taste fantastic," I said around a bite. "Even without chocolate chips."

He rolled his eyes, but a hint of a smile lifted his lips before he replaced it with a scowl. "I was cooking for myself."

"And yet you made some for me. Thank you."

He huffed and kept eating.

"Is it hard to be cranky all the time?" I asked.

"Is it hard to be Miss Cheerful all the time?"

"Sometimes, yes. My life has pretty much sucked, but I try to look on the bright side of things whenever I can."

His growly façade popped like a big balloon, fizzling around the room before sagging onto the floor. "What do you mean?"

"Last night, I mentioned my dad and how he's really controlling. If you've got time for a story, I'll share."

He nodded and kept eating, washing bites down with sips of coffee.

I did the same, focusing on my plate because it would be easier to tell him if I couldn't see his reaction. "I shouldn't feel embarrassed to share. I'm twenty-six years old. Yet this is the first time in my life I've felt free, like I get to choose what I do next, who I'm with, and maybe even plan a future outside of his strict control."

"He sounds like a real asshole."

My laugh snorted out. "Totally. Mom died when I was eight. Things were great before that, but her death changed him. He was hurt, but all he could focus on was himself. His loss was it. It didn't occur to him that I'd lost a mom and was grieving too. I guess you could say he's a narcissist, though that's my uneducated guess."

He frowned and nudged his chin to my plate. I'd stopped eating, setting my fork on my napkin.

I took a bite and spoke around it. "Instead of finding comfort in still having a daughter, all he could talk about was how much he needed my mother. I felt like I mourned alone. I don't have brothers or sisters, and my parents were only children too. If I have grandparents, I never met them. Dad lives in his condo castle on the top floor of a high-rise in a big city, and he never lets anyone enter his home outside of business."

"It sounds lonely for you."

"So much." I sighed. "I had imaginary friends. They talked to me. And I had the internet and TV, so I wasn't completely isolated." I swallowed, but my bite didn't want to go down. "I made lots of friends online."

Was that why I'd fallen so hard and fast for the person I thought was Ryett? He was kind, and he'd listened. He'd told me I had worth, that I was special.

And all this time it was his mother.

Did I have enough time to show *Ryett* I was special?

"You must've gone to school," he said, finishing his meal and placing his fork carefully on his syrupy plate.

"Dad hired someone to teach me."

"Was she a friend?"

"She was." I smiled, remembering Maryjane. "She taught me the basics, though I quickly advanced very far with math. She said I had true potential. She expanded my world. When she was there, I learned about biology and anatomy. She showed me what it might be like to live in Paris and Italy. On the internet, we visited Pompeii and strode through the streets of Marrakech. I can still taste the mint tea and Chicken B'stilla we made together. B'stilla is a kind of chicken pie with a flaky crust. It's yummy."

"I'm glad you had her." He studied my face, and I sensed he wanted to touch me, even soothe me, but I also sensed he didn't know how.

When he was changed, had he closed himself off to everyone around him other than his mom? If so, he'd locked himself inside the same way my dad had done with me, closing me off to almost everything fun and wonderful in life.

We may have more in common than he believed. I'd chosen the sun while he hid with the moon.

Could we bring our worlds together to create one?

"My father told her I'd learned enough when I turned seventeen," I said. "I didn't see Maryjane again." Her loss left a gaping hole inside me no one had filled since, like I'd lost my mom all over again.

"And then you were alone," he said. "No college?"

"He said I didn't need it, that my future role was to be a good wife. He paraded one guy after another in front of me, and I guess I can be grateful that he allowed me some say in who I might marry."

"You didn't marry any of them," he snarled.

"As much as I wanted to escape the cage he'd put me in, I didn't want to fly out the door and into another, more permanent trap."

"Instead, you married me."

Did he see this as another trap? I didn't. I shrugged. "You were my choice, not his. He got impatient with me constantly saying no and told me he'd made a selection, and I'd marry his choice in three months. That's when I saw that you were looking for a mail-order bride." I held up my hand before he could speak. "I know you didn't place the ad, but something about it made me take a second look."

"What did my mother say?"

"That you lived alone, that you worked hard, and that you were lonely."

He stood abruptly and snatched his plate off the counter, stacking it fast with the others before pivoting and striding over to the sink. The plates clinked in the basin, and he ran water over them before putting them in the dishwasher, not turning my way. "My mom shouldn't have done that."

"But she did, and here we are." Why didn't he bring up the sexual things we'd done? I might be naïve and incredibly foolish, but I didn't believe he'd done those things to placate me. He'd been solely focused on my pleasure. If he was the type who'd use me, he would've fucked me already.

He finished loading the dishes into the dishwasher and started it up. "I have to do that stuff outside." Heading to the door, he tugged his coat off a peg beside it, not looking my way. "I'll be back later."

"I'll help," I said, sliding off the stool and grabbing my jacket from the peg next to his. Ha. His and her pegs. Like he'd see it that way?

Did he think he could pretend everything hadn't happened as long as he didn't see me?

I still held out hope I could draw out the Ryett hidden in his mom's messages. It would sound stupid to anyone else, but the person she'd shown me existed in him.

"You'll get wet," he said.

"So will you."

"Just don't get in my way." He wrenched open the door and a blast of water and wind hit us.

Chapter 15
Ryett

Her story made me feel sad for her. I pictured a lonely kid living in a stone tower with only the view of a big, cold city.

She was too much like me, locked inside without a way to get free.

Seeing how similar we were was like claws scraping across my soul. I bled for her, felt for her, just like I had myself after I was changed.

It was all I could do not to tug her into my arms and hold her. She was wiggling her way into my heart much too quickly, and I didn't like it. It was safer to keep myself locked up. If she left me, it would hurt more than when my friends and most of my family rejected me.

"What are we going to do outside?" she shouted to be heard over the rush of the wind.

What a crapshoot. This storm had come out of nowhere, barreling through the surrounding mountain range and trapping everyone inside the valley.

"I have to make sure everything's secure," I bellowed back.

Her nod told me she'd heard. I'd feel better if she stayed inside where it was safe. I didn't mind risking my life out here, but hers was precious.

No!

I couldn't think of her that way. Alright, it *was* precious. To someone.

Maybe me.

Damn my mother for getting me into this. And damn me for starting to think I'd be foolish not to keep Nettie.

"Stay close behind me," I growled, irritated with myself for softening.

Maybe a wife wouldn't be too bad, as long as it was this one. I could picture us sitting on the sofa together in the evening. Making foods that *did not* have chocolate chips in them. Climbing into bed together when the day was through. I'd make sure she found pleasure every moment in her life, not surround her with sadness like her father.

She grabbed onto my jacket and pressed her forehead into my back. "Blustery out here!"

"Don't get lost."

"I won't."

Would it be such a bad thing to admit my mom was right, that I needed someone in my life other than her?

No, that I needed Nettie?

I couldn't figure out something like that while tackling this storm. Maintaining focus would keep us both from being hurt. It would slice through me if Nettie got injured.

Letting my mind start thinking me and Nettie could have something lasting would only result in me being hurt. She was leaving as soon as the storm ended, and I'd say goodbye before turning away and stepping back into the life I had before I knew she existed.

As we made our way across my driveway to the two-story barn I'd built last summer, the wind battered us. I bent into it, ignoring the rain getting in my hair, eyes, and saturating my clothing despite my jacket. It wasn't cold; this was a tropical storm that somehow made its way to this part of the country.

I had to make sure it hadn't done any damage.

When we reached the barn, I shouldered open the door and clung to the panel when the wind would've snatched it from my hand and slammed it against the outside wall.

I waved to the interior.

She hurried inside ahead of me, and I wrangled the door back into place, making sure the latch secured.

"Whoa," she said, pushing her wet hair off her face. She pulled a hair tie from her pocket and secured the gorgeous tresses in a scrunched-up thing at her nape. Tying it down was a true crime. I'd barely resisted burying my face in the silky strands last night.

She peered around, taking in the old Jeep I was slowly restoring parked in the middle, the open loft above where I'd store hay if I ever got animals, plus the stalls lining the outer sides of the first floor. "This is cool."

"I built it myself." I shouldn't feel pride that she admired my work.

She moved over to the bright red Jeep, tapping the hood. "Does it run?"

"Of course it does," I said. Strange that I had to force the snarl. It was almost like I wanted to speak softly and kindly to her all the time.

I needed to rip that shit out of my soul like a weed.

I raked my hands across my horns, remembering how good it felt when she stroked them last night. I wanted her to do it again while I drove myself inside her. It was too easy to picture her legs hooking around my ass. Her heady sighs echoing around us.

My damn cock liked this fantasy and started stiffening.

"It's really cool," she said, peering through the driver's window. "I assume you take the top and doors off in the summer."

"Yeah." I followed her, unable to start the tasks I'd come here to do. "It's a 1986, the first year they made Wranglers like this. The color's metallic garnet, which I kept true when I had it repainted. You should've seen it when I hauled it out of that junkyard. But I fixed all the rusty places, and I was lucky the underside was in decent shape."

"I love it." She shot me a smile through the plastic back window. "I can picture us riding into town, or maybe on some old logging roads with the top down."

For that, she'd still have to be here when the storm was over.

And I hadn't decided if she should.

Chapter 16
Nettie

"I need to look around outside," he said after he'd scoured the interior of the barn from top to bottom. No leaks in the roof and the plank siding appeared secure. "I want to make sure nothing's been damaged by the storm."

"Okay."

We bared the weather once more.

As he secured the barn doors, I peered around, taking in the trees swaying in the wind and water running down the driveway, creating channels in the soft soil.

"I'll go with you to the house," he said, taking my hand and tugging me over to the steps and up onto the deck. "Go inside and get dry. I won't be long." He left me before I could speak.

What if I didn't want to go inside? Maybe I wanted to help him with whatever wouldn't take long.

I scowled as he strode past the barn and started up a

long slope toward the forest looming at the back of the property.

He paused by the back corner of the barn and looked my way. I could feel his glare scorching my skin.

When I reached for the door, he rounded the barn, heading out of sight.

Leaving the porch, I crept after him. I'd slink behind him and make sure he was okay. What if he slipped and fell? Injured, he might lie on the ground for hours. If I was with him, I could help him get up, take him inside, and bandage any wounds.

I'd do anything to make sure he was safe.

While the wind churned around me and the rain pummeled my back, I tiptoed along the barn. At the corner, I paused, listening, but the storm was too ferocious to hear anything.

A peek around the corner revealed shadowy shapes between the barn and another building built close to the woods.

Since I didn't see him, he must've gone inside the building.

I scooted in that direction.

With the rain slamming into me from all sides, it was hard to see where I was going.

And that's why I almost ran into the bear.

Chapter 17
Nettie

I screamed. "Wa! Bear!" Flailing backward, I tripped and landed hard on my ass. I scrambled to my feet, my wide eyes taking in the enormous creature.

It loomed over me, its vicious claws extended to rip me to shreds.

Another beast raced toward me from the right. They'd surround me and eat me alive.

Shrieking, I spun to run back down the hill, only to have the second creature wrap its arms around me.

"Nettie," Ryett yelled by my ear. "It's me."

Twisting, I leaped onto him. "Bear. Bear! Run. Get away. I'll distract it."

He chuckled, and if I wasn't clinging to him like a burdock to a wool sock, I wouldn't have heard his humor over the wind.

Leaning back in his arms, I peered at his face. "Is the bear your pet?"

"You could say that." He held me easily, not putting me down. "There's no real bear."

"I saw one. It was coming after me."

"The only bear in the vicinity won't harm you."

He turned and carried me uphill. "Allow me to introduce you to the ferocious beast." Stopping in front of the looming bear, he said nothing.

"It's . . . not real." I reached out a tentative hand to touch it, encountering wood. "It's a statue."

"It is. There are others about, so if you're going to keep disobeying me and following, you'll need to watch out for them."

I wiggled until he put me down. "I was watching out for *you*. You could've fallen and broken your leg or hit your head."

"What would you do if something like that happened?" He cocked his head, watching me.

"Help you into the house where I could nurse you."

He chuckled, and the joyous sound tickled down my spine, sliding into my bones to take root. "I appreciate it, but I'm fine. No falls. No broken bones. No cracks in the head." He extended his hand toward me. "Would you like to meet the other vicious beasts?"

For a moment, I stood there stunned while the rain continued to drench me. He was suggesting I hold his hand?

I wasn't dumb. I took it and sidled close to his side. Warmth radiated off his body, enfolding me like an embrace. Even better, he'd shucked his jacket, wrapping it around his waist. His left wing wrapped around me, sheltering me, and I closed my eyes for a second, sucking in the wonderful feeling of being protected by Ryett.

He took me from one to the next. Most were sheltered beneath the trees and somewhat out of the wind.

"Where did they come from?" I asked as he led me through his silent forest made up of wooden statues.

"I made them."

"You carved them?" I asked in awe.

"You'd be surprised what a guy can do with a chainsaw. I fell the trees, kiln dry them, then try to imagine what shape the tree would like to take. With the saw, I make the big cuts, then switch to smaller saws to do the detail work."

"Where did you learn to do this?" I stared in amazement at a big, dusky green orc, his tusks bared. He held an enormous hammer. Wearing only a loincloth, he stared toward the woods, and even in the dim light, I could see the longing in his eyes. A female orc dressed in what looked like a Disney princess outfit stared up at him with a big grin and though they were of the same species, I suspected they weren't lovers or mates.

"My friend, Gunner, and his sister, Poppy," Ryett said, leading me past the orcs and a golden-skinned ogre. "I take inspiration from the world—and people—around me. And to answer your question, I taught myself."

"You're so clever."

"I was alone a lot. It was something to do." He watched me as I studied each of his pieces of art. Did he think I'd mock him or be unable to see how gorgeous his art was?

We passed a Frankenstein-like guy lumbering across the lawn on stiff legs with his arms extended, a Valkyrie and a gargoyle, the latter hunched over as if it was poised on the edge of the roof, surveying everything around it.

Ryett stopped his tour at the door to the small building. "I have a few more things inside. Stuff I'm still working on. Want to see?" He didn't look my way, and the tension in his body told me he still expected rejection.

I spontaneously hugged him from behind, wrapping my arms around him as far as they would reach. It felt good to press my cheek against his wings. While he stood stiffly, I sucked in his warmth. His wings were softer than they appeared, almost rubbery and coated with tiny bronze hairs.

"I want to see everything, Ryett," I whispered, unsure he'd hear. I was rapidly falling for him, and I couldn't seem to hold myself back.

When he sent me away, I was going to crash hard and fast, but I accepted it.

At least I'd know love.

Even if it was never returned.

Chapter 18
Ryett

I couldn't believe I wanted to show Nettie my work. Even my mom didn't know much about it. I'd thought of telling her, but I wasn't sure what she'd say. When she saw the statues, I told her a friend did them, that I was an avid collector.

Easing away from Nettie wasn't easy, so I took her hand, pretending that she might lose her footing, and I wanted to make sure she wouldn't fall. I suspected neither of us believed that.

She was creeping past my walls, and I couldn't figure out how to hold her back. It wasn't just her exterior, though I craved her lush body. Her kindness shone through, like a blinding light in a harsh world gone completely dark.

That was me, the harsh world. Would I step into her light and follow it to her or would I turn my back? I hadn't yet decided.

Shouldering open the door, I urged her inside.

"There's no electricity in this building," I said. "I only work during daylight hours, but I have a big flashlight for the few times I forget what I'm doing and work late. Stay here."

When I stepped away from her, she clung to the side of my coat, inching along with me across the rough wooden floor.

Of course she wouldn't remain where I told her. This woman would either drive me out of my mind or make my life so much better, and I hated the thought that the latter even occurred to me.

I wanted to shove her away emotionally, but I couldn't seem to find the will or the words to do that either.

Grabbing the flashlight off the bench, I clicked it on, shining it at the floor to give her eyes a chance to adjust.

Then I took her on a tour, watching her more than where I was going.

"A troll," she said, stooping down to carefully touch the gnarly green face. She smiled at me. "They're all amazing. You've got true talent."

I grumbled, unsure of what to say. Sure, people found my website and bought my sculptures, paying more than I could've ever imagined. Many sent me complimentary messages, but they were strangers. Their words felt distant, as if they were sent to someone other than me.

Nettie admiring my work made my heart pound.

"I just do this to keep from being bored," I said.

She straightened and took my hand much too easily. I'd shown her it was okay by doing it myself. "They're incredible." She tugged me over to a stately elf staring down his nose at us, then on to a delicate fairy crouched on a flower. "Look at her face. She's full of mischief."

"She looks like someone I know in town." I swept my arm out. "All of them are friends from around the area or solely from my imagination. I craft my creatures, taking huge logs and turning them into monsters like me."

"Changing the wood like the potion changed you."

"Something like that." This woman saw too much, felt too much. She kept poking and prodding, and if I wasn't careful, I'd bare my soul to her.

Then she'd reject me like nearly everyone else had.

"This looks like . . ." She stared back and forth between a statue I'd recently finished and me. "A self-portrait, so to speak?" Her breath caught when she spied the second one standing in the shadow of the first. "Oh, there are two of them. But you said you're an only child. Were other wyverns created from the brew?"

"No, I'm the only one." I tapped the shoulder of the first, who scowled at the world around him. "I call this one Angry."

"And the other looks relaxed, happy even."

"Yeah, that's his name—so far."

Turning, she studied my face. "Which one of them is you?"

She was much too perceptive.

Still, I couldn't hold the words back. "I haven't decided yet."

Chapter 19
Nettie

We left his shop.

As we wove among his statues, I kept marveling at how amazing his art was. I wanted to keep raving about his work, but it was obvious by how quickly his eyes shuttered that my gushing made him uncomfortable.

"I have to check the driveway," he said. "Make sure it's clear."

"I'll help."

He grumbled, but he didn't try to make me go inside again.

As we passed the barn, I spied branches lying against the back wall, fallen from a nearby maple.

He hauled the larger ones over to the woods while I cleared away the smaller pieces.

"This one's too big to drag," he said, laying his palm on a limb as thick as my thigh. "Wait here, and I mean it this time."

I rolled my eyes but did as he asked.

He returned with a chainsaw and started it up. Its low rumble turned into a hefty scream as he deftly sliced through the limb, quickly turning it into pieces I stacked near the back of the barn. Firewood for next winter, I presumed. Did he split it himself or use a machine? I could picture him stripped down to almost nothing, his muscles gleaming in the sunlight as he hefted the ax overhead and brought it down onto the wood with a sharp crack.

Would I be here then, or would I only be a distant memory to Ryett?

It hurt that he might not want me. I was still determined to keep trying to show him we had potential, but my efforts may be in vain. When the storm was over, he might still take me to town and put me on a bus to a city where I'd have to start over.

While I covered my ears, he finished cutting the limb. The wind kept shooting me in various directions, and the rain trickling down my spine was unpleasant, bringing out my shivers.

There was no place I'd rather be than here, helping Ryett.

Once we'd cleared all the branches from around the barn, and we'd finished stacking the logs, he returned the chainsaw to where he'd collected it inside.

"Now the road," he yelled to be heard above the wind.

Storm clouds skittered across the sky, dark and heavy with rain. I'd never imagined weathering such fury. I should be scared something terrible would happen. Instead, I felt giddy because I was with Ryett.

I was falling for my proxy husband, and I couldn't seem to hold my emotions in check. Sure, he was grumpy and snarly, but I still saw the guy inside I'd imagined during each of our precious email conversations. Would that guy claw his way to the surface before he sent me away?

I clung to his coat while we walked down the steep driveway where the rain had half washed away. Deep channels had flooded on either side where a vehicle's tires would go. Good thing he had a four-wheel-drive Jeep.

We cleared more trees from the track, then slogged our way back up the hill to his cabin, stomping inside.

"Strip," he said as he secured the door.

Oh, how I wish he'd say that with overwhelming lust in his voice.

I heeled off my shoes and hung my coat on the peg next to his. They looked nice there together, but I snapped at my heart to stop it. If I wasn't careful, I'd shatter when the storm ended, and he said it was time to take me to town.

Where would I go from there?

Not back to my dad. Thankfully, I'd hidden money away through the years. I had enough to start over. I wasn't afraid to work, and I'd taken my social security card from the safe when Dad left it open once.

Plus, I had Mom's jewelry, something Dad ignored after she died. I'd hate to sell it, but she'd had a thing for diamonds my father indulged in. Her final gift to me would give me enough to start over.

"Bathroom or bedroom?" I asked, keeping my voice neutral despite my fluttering insides that felt anything but neutral about Ryett.

He leveled me a look I couldn't quite define. If I didn't know better, I'd think his eyes smoldered.

Smoke coiled from his nostrils, but I'd seen that before, so I wasn't startled.

"I could also strip here." I reached for the hem of my saturated t-shirt, but my fingers stalled. I waited to see what he'd say or do.

His gaze moved down my body in what felt like a heavy caress. My nipples had perked up due to my saturated clothing, but now they throbbed, standing at attention, eager for his touch.

Even my leggings clung to my thighs.

More smoke chugged from his nostrils, enough I worried he'd set himself and me aflame.

I was aflame already. My body ached with need. I wanted to peel off my clothing and climb all over him.

He reached toward my breasts with both hands, but his fingers stopped before touching. A groan ripped through him, and more smoke churned from his nose, clouding around us. Instead of making me cough or sneeze, I sucked it in. It smelled sweet and spicy, like him.

Smoke billowed up above us as he groaned again. He laid his hands on my breasts, cupping them, squeezing them while stroking his thumb claw across my nipples.

He stepped closer, and his wings flared out before wrapping around me. I'd never felt so cherished in my life.

I tipped my head back, watching his face. More smoke shot from his nostrils, and it lit my senses on fire, coiling around me and making my core ache for him.

His head lowered. "I can't resist you any longer, Nettie. I need you."

"I'm yours." A storm and family interference might've brought us together, but we'd been destined forever. We would've found each other because it would be a tragedy for us to live apart. We'd be half what we—

An alarm blared, making my eardrums rattle.

His eyes shot to the ceiling.

"I set the smoke detector off." He actually chuckled. "That hasn't happened since I was fifteen. Wait here?"

At my nod, he took flight, soaring up to the second story ceiling where he yanked the cover off the smoke detector and pulled out the battery. He did the same with the others before returning to stand in front of me, his wings folding back onto his spine.

He shot me a look full of vulnerability. I couldn't breathe through the tightness in my throat.

"Good thing I haven't finished wiring them into the panel, huh?" he said.

My eyes stung from tears, but I jerked out a nod.

He held open his arms, and his wings unfurled once more.

I stepped close to him, and he enfolded me in everything wonderful in this world.

Turning with me in his arms, he raced toward the bedroom.

Chapter 20
Ryett

Once the floodgates opened and my emotions poured out, I could no more resist Nettie than I could flying. She was a visceral part of my soul, and I worried there'd be no wrenching her away without severing something vital inside me.

I carried her to my bedroom and set her on her feet. "I'm going to take your clothing off, shred my own to get out of them, and then I'm going to lay you on my bed and love you."

At her nod, I tugged up her saturated shirt, carefully working it over her head. I tossed it aside and studied her bra.

She unhooked it at the back, and the material shifted forward.

I slipped it off, being gentle with her arms, and threw her bra away. It smacked against the wall and slithered down onto the floor.

Her breasts were large and round, with big nipples

surrounded by darker skin. I'd die if I didn't get to taste them.

"You're beautiful, Nettie," I growled, unable to believe this woman was here in my home, willing to be with me for now and maybe always. I stroked her breasts, cupping them from beneath, running the pads of my thumbs across her nipples.

She arched her spine, thrusting her breasts forward, pressing them into my palms.

I bent over and sucked one into my mouth, groaning at how wonderful it was, how wonderful *she* was. Why had I resisted this, her?

She moaned and tipped her head back and that was all it took to break the bindings I'd placed on my soul.

I eased her pants off and then her panties, pausing to push my face between her thighs. She smelled like heat and fire and everything wonderful. I planned to taste her all night.

Like I said I'd do, I ripped through my shirt and pants, letting the pieces fall to the floor.

"If you do that too often, you'll have to run around naked," she said with a grin. "I approve, however. There's something incredibly sexy about you clawing through your clothing because you want to press your body against mine."

More smoke coiled from my nostrils, and while it had happened before, I'd never churned out so much this fast. It wasn't true smoke, more like my essence, if that made sense.

I really needed to read up some more on wyverns. I'd

always assumed I was still human beneath my wyvern suit, but what if this beast sunk all the way through me?

I wasn't a guy who was good with words. I tended to communicate with growls and grunts. I'd denied this woman when she arrived here. I'd acted surly and maybe even mean.

"I'm going to make it up to you, Nettie," I growled, still not able to fully toss aside everything that made me who I was today.

"Then get to it," she quipped.

Barreling into her, I took us both down onto the bed, taking care not to crush her. With my wings wrapped around her, I rolled, coming to a stop with my thighs straddling her hips, my wings beneath her. She looked good wrapped up in me, and if I had any say in it, here was where she'd stay.

I kissed her, savoring the delicious way she wiggled beneath me. When I'd licked her, I'd nearly come without a single touch on her part. Now, my cock throbbed, needy thing that it was. I couldn't wait to sink inside her.

As we kissed, I moved my palm down her body, kneading and stroking, bringing out her sighs. When I nudged her thighs apart and stroked her saturated flesh, she bucked up against my fingers, moaning. Her head thrashed, and her eyelids slid closed.

"Ryett," she cried, latching onto my horns.

I kissed down her neck, stopping to nibble on the flesh above her collarbone. Her succulent breasts called to me, and there was no denying their cry. I sucked on one nipple after another while stroking her wet folds and running the pad of my thumb across her clit.

She moaned and bucked against me, pushing toward my fingers. I slid one inside her and groaned, nearly coming on the spot. This woman heated me up like no other, though I hadn't been with many. Once I discovered the few I slept with did so because they thought it would be fun to be with a wyvern, I gave up on having someone in my life.

I gave up on love.

"I want you," Nettie growled, clinging to my horns. Jerking on them, and it felt amazing. Each tug sent electricity to my cock, making it surge upward.

I tugged my fingers out of her, and man, did I hate doing it. Watching her responses to my touch dragged through my emotions like a rake, stirring them up. I wasn't sure I liked *feeling*.

Rising over her, I nudged her thighs further apart. She lifted her legs, hooking them on my hips. She stared right at me, making me hold her gaze.

A sense of vulnerability flashed through me, but I couldn't look away. Not when I placed the head of my cock at her entrance.

And not when I pushed forward, burying myself inside her.

Chapter 21
Nettie

He plunged into me, and I groaned. Such exquisite pleasure. It was all I could do not to come. Coming would be awesome, but I wanted to ride this out with Ryett.

Who knew if this would change things for us? I had now, and I'd drink from it what I could.

He pulled out and drove himself inside me again, his gaze locked on mine. The loneliness I'd seen from the moment I arrived had been replaced with pure lust, plus a hint of something I couldn't define.

If I didn't know better, I'd think he felt something for me. Caring? No, it was something more.

Not wanting to analyze anything other than the size of his cock and how amazing its thick length felt surging inside me, I wrenched my gaze from his and focused on feeling.

Each time he pulled back and pushed forward again,

I rocked my hips up to meet him. He reached between us and ran his fingertips across my clit.

"More of that, and I'm going to explode," I grunted out.

"Do it. Come. Explode," he growled, pushing harder on my clit and pistoning his hips faster. "I want to feel your body sucking on my cock, Nettie."

That was all it took. My mind shot upward, spinning and coiling. And when it released, my body did too. Shudders took over my frame, and I clung to him as he rode me through it.

Only when I returned to the moment did he push harder, groan louder, and let his own orgasm consume him. He went faster, slamming into me, driving me into another spiral that roared through me like a freight train.

When he collapsed on top of me, I held him, stroking his back.

I savored how good it felt to be held in his arms.

I woke during the night to him slipping from the bed.

I reached out to him; I couldn't help it.

"I won't be long," he whispered. "The power went out. I need to get wood and light the stove in the living room, or we'll get cold."

Outside, the wind continued to howl. What kind of storm stalled and pummeled one area for so long? This one, I supposed.

"I'll help." I tossed the covers back and dressed quickly in dry clothing, stuffing my feet into my sneakers.

He waited in the kitchen, pacing in the dim light generated by an emergency flashlight now running on battery power. "You should go back to bed." Reaching out, he stroked a few strands of hair off my face. "Keep it warm for me."

"I think we can warm things up nicely once we're done bringing in wood. It's stacked along the side of the barn, right?" I'd noted a big pile covered with a tarp.

"I don't want you to do things like that."

Ah, there was that growl again. "Did you know that turns me on?"

He paused in his pacing. "What does?"

"When you growl at me, I get all tingly and my clit throbs."

"Nettie," he snarled.

"That too. The snarl." My grin slipped out. "Keep doing it, will ya? Then, by the time we've brought in the wood and lit the fire, I'll be climbing all over you."

"What am I going to do with you?" he snapped, yanking his jacket off the peg. He did the same with mine, tossing it to me.

"I think you know very well what you're going to do with me."

Chapter 22
Ryett

I was falling in love with my mail-order bride, and I couldn't stop it from happening.

Wrenching open the back door, I held it for Nettie, then passed her, stomping down the back stairs. I swept my flashlight's beam back and forth, looking for that green reflection that would indicate predators lurked nearby. I didn't expect many beasties to leave their dens during a storm, but deep in the woods, you could never be too careful.

Other than spooking a deer nibbling on the lawn way back by the woods, I didn't see anything.

"I don't want to love you," I growled at Nettie.

"I can understand that," she shouted above the roar of the wind. Rain pelted us again. Would it ever stop? I'd begun to believe it would pour for the rest of my life. I'd remain locked in my cabin with Nettie, and by the time we could get out, I wouldn't want to let her go.

What if I clung, and she pushed me away?

Shit, I didn't need crap like that.

I didn't need her.

Or did I?

When she stumbled over something, I latched onto her arm, tugging her into my side and wrapping my wing around her. I curled it over her head, giving her a bit of shelter.

"I'm not sure I want to love you either," she bellowed back, snuggling against me as we made our way up the hill toward the barn.

I snarled.

She shot me a grin and wiggled her eyebrows. When she licked her lips, I groaned and tugged her even closer, lifting her so I could greedily latch onto her mouth.

She moaned and wrapped her legs around me. I lost my grip on my flashlight. If it hadn't fallen on my foot, I would've pressed her against the side of the barn and hump her.

That wasn't such a bad idea.

With her clinging to me like a leech and my lips locked on hers, I stumbled the rest of the way to the barn and beneath the overhang that gave us decent shelter. I backed her against the side and tore at her clothing, then my own. In no time, we were naked. Rain swept beneath the overhang, pummeling us, but if she noticed, she didn't say a word.

Me? I was too damn lost in the feel of her flesh beneath my palms and the heady sound of her moans to care.

She spread her legs wider, rubbing her clit against my cock as I ground it against her.

In no time, I was inside, wallowing in her saturated passage that milked me in a way no one ever had or ever would.

Smoke coiled around us, generated by my over-whelming need to consume her.

"Fast," she cried, her head tilting back. "I need it. Now!"

Who could deny a plea like that?

I drove myself into her, pushing hard and swiveling my hips to hit her inner walls in a different way with each thrust.

I slipped my tail between us, laying it on her clit. When I shifted it back and forth, a shriek stuttered from deep inside her. She shattered, giving in to the pleasure I handed right to her.

Unable to hold back, I joined her in bliss, pushing deep and hard, taking her fast.

When we'd both stopped shuddering, I just stared at her. Watched her as she watched me.

"See?" she said, though she didn't smile. "Just keep growling."

Chapter 23
Nettie

My knees quivered as I loaded my arms with wood and carried it into the house. It took three trips to fill the wood box beside the fireplace.

No wonder pioneers needed to eat so much; they burned through everything they ate just staying warm. I couldn't imagine doing this all winter long, then cutting more and stacking it during the summer. Wood heated you through more than once.

"Enough?" I asked, breathing hard.

"Aw, Nettie," he said, tugging me into his arms.

Outside, we'd wrangled back into our wet clothing. It clung to my skin, but I didn't care. Being held by him was all that mattered.

He smelled like the wood we'd carried, the sex we'd had against the side of the barn, and something unfamiliar but spicy and addicting. The last could come from the smoke still coiling from his nostrils. Was he aware it worked like an aphrodisiac on me?

"You shouldn't have carried any of it." Lifting me, he took me over to the sofa, though he placed me on my feet beside it. He stripped off my shirt and pants, using the tender touch of a doting parent. Lifting me again, he deposited me on the cushions and covered me with a pile of blankets so thick I'd have difficulty sucking in a deep breath.

"Are you going to join me?" I asked, holding up the blankets, showing him there was room.

"I will, but not now." He smoothed my hair and slid his fingers carefully along my cheeks. "Do you need a drink? Can I get you a snack?"

"I'm okay." Frankly, I was a bit stunned by how he was behaving, and I was tempted to ask him if aliens had stopped in when I blinked and switched him out with a different model.

Returning to the woodstove, he crumpled newspaper, stuffing it into the opening on the front, adding kindling. After shifting the damper on the black pipe above the stove, he lit the fire and closed the door.

"This should keep us warm enough," he said, wiping his hands. Turning, he leaned against the stove, something he wouldn't be able to do once the cast iron heated. "I should install a generator, but I keep putting it off."

"They cost a fortune." So I'd read. I didn't have personal experience.

"I can afford it, but I hate having people here."

"I got that impression already." Now that we were

getting closer, I could smile. "You were damn intimidating at first."

"But now I make your clit throb." His lips twitched upward before smoothing. Did he realize the smoke coiling from his nose gave him away?

He wanted me. I could work with it.

"Nothing's better than a throbbing clit," I said.

Frowning, he cocked his head. "Is it doing it now?"

"Maybe snarl a bit, and we'll see what happens."

"You're distracting me," he said.

"You love that about me."

His breath caught and his eyes shuttered. Oh, yes, he'd already pointed out that he didn't want to love me.

We'd see about that. I was in love with him, and if nothing else, I never gave up, not until the proverbial ship had sunk in deep waters.

Or the storm was over.

Stalking over to me, he braced his hands on the sofa on either side of my head. "What should I do with you?" he snapped.

"My clit and other parts of me have a few suggestions."

"Nettie," he breathed, the warning and snarl gone from his voice. "I don't want to fall for you."

"Is that something you can control?"

"Maybe." His gaze focused on my mouth. "And maybe not."

One kiss, and he lit me on fire.

Chapter 24
Ryett

If I didn't back away, I was going to tug off the blankets and climb all over Nettie. She wanted me to. From the way she clung to the tips of my wings and the way her mouth parted with a sigh; she'd give herself to me if I so much as curled my finger.

Knowing this formed a crack in my heart. I'd have to get away from her and seal it up or it would widen, and she'd step inside. I'd never get her out after that.

I ripped myself away from her, growling at myself. Wiping my mouth, I stared down at her, taking in the limpid look in her eyes and her puffy lips I ached to kiss once more.

"I need to go check out the power situation," I said, trying to inject a snarl in my voice but unable to find the will. She was tearing away at that, too, and I couldn't seem to stop her. "See if I can fix it."

"Do you know how to work on it?"

I wanted to be irritated by her question, but the

concern on her face popped my snarls like a knife on a balloon, fizzling it before I could gather up the shreds. "I'll figure it out."

"I'm not afraid of you snarling or growling," she said calmly. "As I've said, that turns me on. But I just want you to be safe."

She started to shift the blankets to the side, but I tugged them back into place, all the way up to her chin. If I covered her delectable body, I wouldn't be tempted to strip off my clothing, part her thighs, and delve into her sweetness.

I backed away fast, stalking across the room and grabbing my wet jacket from beside the door. "I want you to remain here."

"Can I do anything while you're gone?"

"Not really. Don't run the water or flush the toilet. There's a bit of water in the line from the well, but once that runs out, the pump won't work to pull more. If I can find the problem and fix it, we'll be back in business. I've put aside gallons of water in the kitchen cabinet. We'll drink those."

"Do you have candles or lanterns I can light?"

A tremor came through in her words. I pinched my eyes shut. I should leave the house. Hell, hide in the woods until the storm ended.

Instead, I paced back to Nettie and stooped down in front of her.

Her lower lip trembled, but she lifted a smile that didn't quite reach her eyes.

Just like that, my heart split wide open all over again.

She didn't step into my heart; I drew her close, tugging her inside.

I lifted her with my wings, curling them around her, pressing her into me until I wasn't sure where her heartbeat stopped and mine began. Holding her, I placed my chin on the top of her head.

She nestled into me as if she belonged with me always.

I was beginning to suspect she did.

Did I dare tell her? It would be easier to let her go once the storm was over. Then I could patch up my heart and move on with my life.

I didn't want to be alone any longer. My mom loved me, but it wasn't the same thing.

My mother had seen it before me.

I couldn't be angry with her for acting when I hadn't dared. She loved me, and she wanted me to be happy.

Nettie shifted. "I'm sorry," she said against my chest.

"For what?" Overcome with emotion, my voice croaked.

"Being frightened when I shouldn't be. For clinging."

"We all do it every now and then."

She tipped her head back and looked up at me. "Not you."

"What makes you think I'm not scared sometimes?"

"You're brave and strong. You could probably tangle with a bear and come up the victor. You were transformed, and I'm sure you weren't happy with what you were turned into, but you seem to have shrugged it aside and found a new place where you fit in."

"I imagine you've done that yourself, Nettie. Look at you, traveling across the country to be with a guy you only met online."

"Most people would say I was out of my mind to do it. You could be a stalker or a serial killer."

I chuckled. "You think I'm not?"

"I know you, Ryett. You grumble and stomp around, but you would never hurt anyone. You won't hurt me."

And in that, she was wrong. I'd done so, and unless I could figure this out, I was going to do it again.

I kissed her forehead and eased her back onto the sofa, making sure she was completely covered with blankets. "I won't be long. Try not to be scared. If you get cold, snuggle up to the woodstove."

Leaving her, I walked toward the door.

"Come back soon," she said. "Be safe. And when you get back, I'll warm *you* up."

Chapter 25
Nettie

Gusts of wind hit the building, but Ryett had built a sturdy home. I bet it could withstand anything.

The drum of rain on the roof was punctuated by the snap of the fire in the stove.

Minutes turned into more minutes, and he didn't return.

Rising, I went to the bedroom and dressed, returning to the living room. I'd clung to him before he left because I was scared something would happen to him, not because I'd be alone. Somewhere between offering to make chocolate chip pancakes and teasing him about making my clit throb with his growls, I'd fallen in love.

Sadly, I wasn't sure he felt the same. I suspected he mostly felt pity.

And I *was* a pitiful thing, a lost woman who'd run from a bad situation and into one that might not be much better. I'd traveled across the country to pursue a dream that had imploded the minute I arrived.

When he told me I had to leave, I'd lift my chin, wish him well, and say goodbye. It would be wrong to force this, to try to make him hand me his heart.

I went to the fridge, contemplating what we could make for dinner, but I didn't want to open it to explore the options. Without power, our food would quickly grow warm. I assumed we should keep the cold inside as long as possible.

Instead, I searched the cupboards, taking out crackers and cans of soup. But without the microwave, I couldn't heat it. The stove was gas, but that also took electricity to ignite.

I wasn't hungry anyway. I just wanted Ryett inside the house with me where I could watch out for him.

Something hit the roof with a big thump, the sound jarring through my bones.

I scurried over to the door and peered through the glass, but the rain was coming down too hard to see.

Cracking the door, I called out. "Ryett?"

The wind started whispering things I didn't want to hear. He'd done something with downed wires and electricity had jolted through him. He's slipped and fallen, breaking his leg.

Right now, he was lying on the saturated ground, unconscious.

Or calling out for help.

I knew this wasn't true.

Or did I?

I shut the door and started pacing back and forth between the kitchen and the living room, pausing in the latter to peer through the glass. Still seeing nothing upsetting, but also not seeing Ryett didn't make things better.

"Stay inside, he said." I whispered. "He'll be upset if I follow. He'll grump and grumble and growl—though I don't mind that."

Despite his surly attitude, he liked me. Could he love me like I did him?

It wouldn't matter if he was lying outside, dying.

"Alright, sneak out and look for him," I said, putting on my sneakers. "Then spy on him, watch out for him, and sneak back inside before he beats you to it."

I put on my coat and grabbed the flashlight. Then I braved the storm to track down the wyvern I loved.

The wind hit me before I'd left the porch, and rain drenched me through—again.

First, I walked around the house, shining the flashlight here and there. I didn't find Ryett, but I did come across a tree limb. That must be what I'd heard hit the roof. It was lying on the ground, not leaning against the house, so I left it, striding toward the barn.

Inside, silence greeted me. "Ryett?"

So much for sneaking up on him and rushing back to the house before he knew I was around.

When he didn't reply, I scoured the barn from top to bottom, but he wasn't there.

Outside, I strode up the hill, weaving among his gorgeous statues until I reached his shop.

He wasn't there either.

I stood at the top of the hill, peering around, but the rain made visibility a challenge.

"The driveway," I whispered. "The power lines must come up the side. I bet I'll find him there, clearing brush." Something I would've gladly helped him with.

If only he saw me as a partner and not someone he had to watch out for until this cursed storm ended.

Actually, it wasn't so cursed if it kept us together. I should want it to last forever.

I headed down the hill and to the driveway. The woods crowded in close, and the ground had washed away in places, making the going treacherous. As expected, I found piles of brush and small tree limbs stacked along the sides.

It wasn't until I was nearly upon the big tree lying across the driveway that I saw it.

And that's when my gaze was drawn to Ryett lying on the ground beneath it. It lay across his belly, and his arms had flopped on top of it. His poor wings lay askew underneath him.

He wasn't moving.

His eyes were closed.

And from where I stood gaping, it didn't look like he was breathing.

Chapter 26
Ryett

I heard her before I saw her.

Sweet Nettie. The woman I'd snarled at and done my best to drive away.

The woman I'd realized I loved.

I'd had time to think while lying here, and the only thing I wanted to do if I could find my way free was to return to her. Hold her. And tell her I wanted her in my life forever.

She dropped beside me, sobbing. "Ryett. Ryett!" Her hands fluttered before she laid them on my shoulders.

She collapsed on my chest, weeping.

I put my arms around her, holding her, wishing I could do more to reassure her.

"You're alive," she cried, lifting to study my face. "You're horribly wounded."

"I don't believe I am. Look." I jerked my shoulder to the rock jutting up from the driveway beside me. Rain had washed away the soil and crushed stone around it, exposing it and creating a small open area beside it. It was the only reason I was still alive.

"The tree crushed you." She stroked my face. "I'm so sorry. I hoped . . ."

"What did you hope for, Nettie?" I watched her face, holding my breath.

"I hoped there was still time for us."

There was too much vulnerability in her eyes. And loneliness. It mirrored the feelings I'd lived with since I was changed into a wyvern.

It didn't have to be this way for either of us, not if we were together. I wanted to be the happy statue, not the angry one.

"Get me out from under this tree." When we were inside, I'd show her how much she meant to me. I wasn't a guy who knew how to use the right words. Whatever skill I might've had in that area had bled away when one person after another rejected me. If my mom hadn't been here for me, I might've fled into the woods, never to be seen again.

Instead, I fled into the woods and found a way to live.

"I can do it," she said with determination. She jumped to her feet and tried to lift the foot-thick tree. For a second, I truly thought she'd do it.

She really did care for me if she could find superhuman strength to rescue me.

"Don't," I barked, then softened my voice. Despite the fact that my grumpy nature turned her on, I didn't want to snarl at her any longer.

I only wanted to love her.

"I can get it off," she said, her wet face cratered with determination.

"I need you to stop, Nettie, and listen to me. If the tree rolls off the rock, it's going to crush me."

"No," she wailed. "I won't let it."

I suspected she'd fling her own body beneath it to keep it from happening. It's what I'd do.

"Before you turn into a lumberjack, I need you to go back to the barn. Remember where we stacked the logs yesterday?"

"Yes."

"Get the wheelbarrow from the barn and load a log a little smaller than that gap on my side of the rock and bring it here."

"Alright. I can do that." Fear threaded through her voice, but her gaze remained resolute. She started up the hill, slipping and nearly falling, but righted herself and turned, calling out over her shoulder as she burst into a run. "I'll be right back."

It took longer than I liked, and I worried the entire time she was gone. What if a tree fell on her? Or she tripped and was seriously injured? It wasn't cold out, but when the body got wet, it lost heat. She would suffer, and I wouldn't be able to help her.

She'd be safer if she left me.

Or would she? Just the little bit she'd shared about her father made anger pour through me. If she left, she'd be alone if he tracked her down.

Here, I could protect her, something I wanted to do

more than anything. Not just protect her, but cherish her, show her life could be much better.

"I'm coming," she huffed, guiding the wheelbarrow down the side of the driveway where grass gave her a bit of traction. When she was level with me, she wheeled it over below the tree. "I'm going to lift the log out and lay it nearby. I assume you want me to put it into the gap between you and the rock, to provide support for the tree to keep it from crushing you."

"That's right."

Her resolve was impressive. She'd taken her fear and used it rather than let it dominate her actions. She'd done the same thing with her father. He'd tried to control her, and she'd kept a level head. She'd sought a way out and when it came, she took it.

It didn't take her long to carefully slide the cut limb into the gap. I breathed a sigh of relief despite still being trapped. My biggest fear was that the tree would shift off the rock and finish falling on top of me.

"Next," I said. "I need you to get the chainsaw and cut the tree so I can shift a smaller length off me."

With a nod, she started up the hill again, reappearing not long after carrying my chainsaw.

"How do I start it?" she asked, staring down at it.

"First, let me tell you what we're going to do. You're going to slice through the tree to the right of where it's lying on the rock."

"Okay."

She moved closer to it. The tree had to be twenty feet long and thick, maybe fourteen inches. If I'd been even a few inches closer to the woods on my side . . . I didn't want to think about that, though I'd need to. If something happened to me, Nettie would be alone. She'd do okay in my home until the storm ended, but she wouldn't have me.

And she'd made it clear she wanted me in her life.

"If you cut above the rock, the tree will remain braced on it," I said. "After that, put down the chainsaw, and we'll talk about what we'll do next."

I went through how to start the saw and how to use it to slice cleanly through the tree, reinforcing basic safety measures she'd need to take. It wasn't going to be easy. I worried the tree would shift or the saw would kick back at her. Or that it would get stuck before she'd sliced through. And if she successfully cut it, I worried that it would roll forward, beyond the branch she'd wedged in the space, and crush my lower legs.

"When you're cutting, I want you to stand back a bit from it. Don't hover over it; extend your arms. You're going to cut with the middle of the saw, not the tip."

"Okay."

"Start your cut on the underside of the tree, moving upward until you're about one third of the way through. Then carefully pull it down and saw from the top. Stand on the upper side of the driveway so that the limb you cut doesn't roll down on top of you." If only I could do this for her.

"I'm ready," she said.

At my nod, she started the saw.

Chapter 27
Nettie

I'd probably never be as proficient as Ryett with a chainsaw. How could I be? He used various saws all the time to craft his sculptures. But this would be the most vital cutting I'd make in my life.

Sweat coiled down my spine, making it itch, and my hands were equally moist. I should've looked for gloves in the barn. I didn't want my hands slipping.

Slicing through a tree was easier than I thought it would be. The saw was heavy, but the blade must be sharp. With a screeching whine, it eased up into the bottom of the tree. I watched what I was doing and tugged the saw down when I'd sliced partway through.

Tightening my grip on it, I gave it more gas and started slicing from the top.

Watching intently, Ryett nodded, and his approval meant a lot to me. I might not be his first—or last—pick for a bride, but I was showing him I could be his equal.

Maybe that's what we needed between us to achieve balance.

When my second cut reached the first, a crack rang out. The section of the tree on my right shifted, dropping and rolling down the driveway a few feet.

The piece lying on the rock rolled, too, starting to fall off the rock.

"No," I jerked the saw to the right, dropping it where the blade couldn't slice me. I latched onto the tree and dug my heels into the soft gravel, keeping it from rolling off the rock.

The rumble of the saw was punctuated by my gasps. A glance at Ryett showed him trying to drag himself uphill, out from beneath the tree.

Keeping a tight grip on the tree, I held the cut edge against my belly.

"On three," I shouted above the sound of the saw. "I'm going to lift it."

"Don't," he said. "You'll hurt yourself. I can get out." His hands clawed at the ground, trying to find purchase.

I squatted, hugged the end of the branch with all the strength inside me, and heaved it upward.

Chapter 28
Ryett

Nettie was Wonder Woman. Someone others would create legends around.

I was the one who wasn't worthy.

With a groan, she lifted the tree enough that I could drag myself up the drive and out from beneath it.

"Let go," I cried out once I was free. "Back away fast."

She released it, and it smacked down onto the rock and bounced, falling onto the drive and rolling a few feet before coming to rest.

Nettie glared at it, her chest heaving, before her gaze shot to me. She raced around the rock and over to me, dropping to her knees beside me. "What's broken?"

"Only my heart."

Her head tilted, and she froze, studying my face.

"How could your heart be broken?"

"I need you, Nettie."

"And I'm here to help you. Do you think you can

walk or get into the wheelbarrow? Then I can push you up to the house and get you inside."

"What I mean is my heart will be broken if you leave me, Nettie," I said. "I want you. Need you. Always."

Her eyes widened, and her lips twitched upward before smoothing. "Then it's a good thing I don't plan to leave." She nodded pertly. Leaning into me, she gave me a quick kiss.

Quick wasn't good enough for me. With a groan, I latched onto her and rolled until she was beneath me. I growled as I nibbled on her jawline.

"You're growling again," she said. "You must be feeling perky."

I'd show her perky.

I claimed her mouth, and our kiss shot through me like lightning, lighting up my insides until I glowed with warmth for her.

She moaned and clung to my shoulders, wrapping her legs around me.

I kissed down her neck to the top of her jacket, and growled again because I couldn't reach more of her skin.

"Are we going to roll around in the mud?" she quipped.

"I thought my growls made your clit throb."

"Oh, they do, but the mud's squishy. If we're going to roll around in it, maybe we should take our clothing off first."

"Let's go home." I levered myself off her and tested my legs, grateful I didn't feel much pain. Nothing appeared to be broken, but I was sure I'd find scraped skin and bruises when I stripped. "Then I can take your clothing off."

"Now you're talking." She sprang to her feet.

"I'm going to lick every inch of your body."

"Huh."

"What does that mean?" I snarled.

"Actions speak louder than words."

With a growl—because I knew she liked it—I swept her up and raced toward the cabin.

Chapter 29
Ryett

I wanted to strip Nettie and drag her into the shower. Lather her body and replace my hands with my mouth. Love her until she was a moaning wreck, eager for me to claim her.

But without power, we had no hot water.

We settled for stripping off our clothing near the back door, and with a bit of water in the sink I warmed after lighting the gas stove with a flame, she wiped my skin clean.

She huffed and sighed as she bandaged the scrapes on my thighs and wings, but truly, all I felt was arousal.

After she'd finished with me, I took my turn with her, and let me say, washing Nettie at the sink wasn't half bad.

Soon, she was moaning, and I was growling along with her.

"Clit throbbing alert," she said in a breathy voice as I

dragged the washcloth between her legs. "You're going to have to do something about this issue."

I chuckled, loving how free it sounded. For the first time since I was changed into a wyvern, I was completely happy.

"I believe I have a cure," I said, lifting her off her feet. I half ran, half flew down the hall and laid her lush form on my bed—*our* bed from now on.

I crawled over her, growling as I kissed her from her mouth to her toes, then started back up. Is it my fault I got stuck when I reached the juncture between her gorgeous thighs?

From her cries of joy, I'd say no.

Because I spread them and with another growl, I started to lick her.

When I woke the next morning, Nettie was already up. I rose and tugged on some boxers, following the rich smell of coffee to the kitchen and her. She was the true magnet, however, not the coffee.

"Did you see?" she asked softly, turning and leaning against the counter.

"See what?"

"The storm's over, and the power's back on." She worried her lower lip still plump from my kisses. "What are we going to do?"

Her searching gaze met mine, and I swore she braced herself. Didn't she know I wanted her to stay?

Probably not, because I'd barely told her. I was going to spend a lot of time making up for not greeting her with open arms.

"I know what I want to do," I said.

"What's that?" She swallowed, and tears shimmered in her eyes.

Aw, I hated that.

Tugging her into my arms, I held her. "I love you, Nettie. Real love, the kind with flowers and romance and me worshiping you every day of my life."

"Ryett," she sighed.

"What I want to do is pour some coffee and sit on the front deck with you in my arms. We'll drink our coffee. And then . . ."

"Then?" Her voice sounds happy, and I'd made that happen. I would keep a smile on her face until the day I died.

"And then I want to come inside and beg you to make me some chocolate chip pancakes."

Chapter 30
Epilogue
Nettie

An older woman walked up the driveway. She must've left her car on the road. When she saw us sitting on the deck—me on Ryett's lap—she stopped. She shielded her face from the sun and stared our way.

"And that, my love," Ryett said. "Is my mother."

"I bet you're mad at her."

"I bet you're mad at her too."

"I should be. She manipulated us. She brought me here under false pretenses. She lied. And yet . . ." I struggled to compose my thoughts in order to get them right. "She did it because she loves you. I have to consider that as well."

His arms tightened around me. "I'd like to go speak to her alone, if you don't mind."

"Of course. She's *your* mom."

He sighed. "It's hard to separate the woman who

stood beside me when no one else did with one who'd do something this underhanded."

"I understand."

He eased me off his lap, and I took his seat. He climbed up onto the rail and leapt off.

My heart jumped up into my throat, though the drop to the ground wasn't far. His wings snapped out, and he soared down to where his mom waited. He landed lightly and tucked his wings back against his spine.

They talked, but I couldn't hear what they said.

His mom cried, cupping her face.

Despite her butting her nose into where it didn't belong, my heart ached for her. What must it be like to love your child so much that you'd do something like this? It was misplaced love, I supposed. Twisted to the point where a person feels they have the right to make decisions for other people. It was wrong, and there may be no moving forward from it.

Yet . . . she clearly loved him. She'd done it because she was worried about him, because she wanted him to be with someone who could love him as much as she did.

If she hadn't done it, I never would've met him.

That would be the true tragedy.

Could I forgive her? That, I didn't know. I wasn't the only one who'd been wronged.

So when they hugged, and he took her hand, tugging her up the hill and onto the deck, I stood and swiped my sweaty palms on my jeans. My heart thrummed heavily, and I wasn't sure what I was going to say.

"Mom, this is Nettie," Ryett said. "Nettie, my mom, Belinda."

I couldn't read how I should respond in his eyes.

That's when I realized I didn't need a guy to show me how to behave. I'd done that with my dad for much of my life, and it was time I stopped.

I was a woman who'd used a chainsaw to cut my love free from a fallen tree. I'd helped him into the house and bandaged his wounds. Soon, I'd make him chocolate chip pancakes and tease him when he told me how much he adored them.

I didn't want to love Ryett and hate his mom. I'd lost my mom when I was little, and I'd forgive her for almost anything if it meant she'd be in my life today. It would be foolish to throw away this chance to start with someone new.

So I held out my arms to her.

When she started to cry again, I stepped toward her.

"Hey," I said, rubbing her arms.

"I'm sorry," she gasped out. "It was wrong of me to do it. I lied and manipulated you and my son."

"Did you do it to be mean?" I asked, my head tilting. I could see so much of him in his mother. The same hair color and chin. And her eyes . . . She was lonely too.

My words shocked away her tears. "Of course I didn't do it to be mean. I love Ryett. I only want to see him happy."

"What if I told you we are happy? What if I thanked you instead of berated you? I wouldn't be here without you." I held my hand out to Ryett, and he took it, squeezing it.

Would he have told her to leave if I wasn't willing to put this behind us? I suspected he would. But then I'd be ripping out part of his heart and tossing it aside. I couldn't do that to him.

This time, when I held out my arms, Belinda stepped into them. She held me, rocked me.

"You're such a sweet person," she finally said. "Thank you."

I hadn't fully forgiven her. That would take time.

I left her and eased into Ryett's arms. His wings enfolded me, and when I looked up into his eyes, I saw approval. Adoration. And love.

I didn't need anything more than that.

I hope you enjoyed Ryett & Nettie's story!

Would you like to read more monsters from me?
Check out my Monsterville, USA Series, starting
with Candy For My Orc Boss
I've included Chapter 1 here.

And if you'd like to read more books
from Monster Between the Sheets,
Season 2, you can find them here.

About the Author

Ava Ross is a two-time *USA Today* Bestselling author who has written numerous titles, all of them featuring sweet and steamy romance. She fell for men with unusual features when she first watched Star Wars, where alien creatures have gone mainstream. She lives in New England with her husband (who is sadly not an alien, though he is still cute in his own way), her kids, and a few assorted pets.

Series by AVA

Mail-Order Brides of Crakair

Brides of Driegon

Fated Mates of the Ferlaern Warriors

Fated Mates of the Xilan Warriors

Holiday with a Cu'zod Warrior

Galaxy Games

Alien Warrior Abandoned

Beastly Alien Boss

Bride of the Fae

Candy For My Orc Boss

**A new life, a new job, a new orc husband . . .
Wait, isn't he supposed to be *my boss*?**

After my ex announces his wedding to someone other than me, I'm eager to leave town. A new life and a new job are just what I need to restore my mojo. On the way to my destination, I stay the night at a hotel where edible unmentionables and a tattooed orc construction worker rock my world. I sneak out the next morning, figuring I'll never see him again.

Until I walk into my new job. That hot orc construction worker?

He's my boss.

He's eager to continue where we left off.

And those symbols on his wrists? According to orc tradition, they mean we're married.

Candy for my Orc Boss is Book 1 in the Monsterville, USA Series. Each book is standalone but is best if read in order. Expect romantic hijinks with monsters, heat, and a happily ever after.

Check out the entire Monsterville world!
Candy for my Orc Boss
Orc Me Baby One More Time
Gargoyles Just Want to Have Fun
Don't Go Knotting My Heart
Whose Bed Have Your Claws Been Under?
Uptown Ogre
Oops, I Elf'd it Again
My Orc-y Breaky Heart
Hold Me Closer, Fiery Phoenix
Who Let the Demon Out?

Get it Now!

Chapter 1
Chastity

If only I hadn't encouraged a gorgeous orc to eat my unmentionables. Well, not exactly eat them. I asked him to lick them.

Because they were cherry.

Not my cherry—I lost that years ago. The panties were the edible cherry kind, and they never should've been taken seriously. Except . . . I invited him to do so much more than lick them, and now I was in major trouble.

Tattooed orc construction worker trouble.

Leave it to me, a woman who'd been cursed with the sweeter-than-angels name of Chastity, to get tipsy on one glass of wine. If that wasn't enough, I'd opened my birthday gag gift of edible undies (thanks, BFF since junior high school, Violet) in front of the muscular orc construction guy sitting next to me at the hotel bar.

Giggling me had channeled a boldness Chastity

didn't possess. I'd waved the garment in the air and brazenly suggested someone needed to eat them.

What a major embarrassment this was. Last night? Let's just say that this was what happened when straight-laced Chastity decided to cut loose and have fun. Of course, I wouldn't have done . . . this, if I wasn't still feeling the pinch from being ditched by my now ex-boyfriend. Three months ago, he announced he was getting married—to someone other than me.

Because it hurt to see them together, I'd quit my job and taken one in a small town far from the place I grew up in. En route, I stopped for the night at a hotel and things went in a new direction from there. Tomorrow, I'd settle into an apartment. I'd start my new job two weeks after that.

I'd generated a lot of excitement with my edible undies proposition. I was popular for the first time in my life.

Two vampires offered to suck my blood through the garment at the same time, and a werewolf had taken one look, howled, and bolted from the bar. More yips erupted outside, reminding me the moon was full tonight.

The most interest came from the orc wearing worn jeans, construction boots, and a snug tee outlining his numerous muscles.

He'd urged me on because he was hot. Or I'd *been* hot. No, I hadn't been hot. I'd been determined to show the world I had worth, that guys found me attractive. My ex had ignored me for too long before his surprise engagement.

And . . . here I was, about to bail on the guy who'd given me the best night of my life. Waiting for him to wake up felt cringy. Sometime during the night, I'd reverted to being plain old Chastity.

Muted sunlight filtered around the edges of the hotel room's curtains, not quite reaching the bed. A panty-dropping, muscular tattooed arm laid across my chest. It tightened, and my orc construction worker snuggled into my side. His lips—asleep lips—spread tingles through me as they brushed from my neck to my collarbone.

Ever since mythical creatures became mainstream, I'd wondered what it would be like to date someone different from me.

Let's just say last night took things a bit further than dating.

I had to get out of here before he woke up or the morning-after conversation could prove awkward. What if I asked for his number, and he didn't want to give it to me? I liked him. I wanted to see him again. But my heart was too soft to take another rejection right now.

If I knew his full name, I could find him online. It was clear his mom had not named him Yes!, More!, or Harder!—the only things I'd been capable of screaming last night.

Heat flooded my face when I remembered how I'd shouted for him to do whatever he'd wanted with me. So unlike the times I'd been with my ex.

The orc shifted closer. He thrust his warm, buck-naked thigh upward, pinning my legs to the bed. He mumbled, his words igniting my nerve endings. The saying that orcs do it better was totally true.

His fingertips brushed across my nipple, and it responded like it hadn't had more action in one night than during the past six months combined.

My nipple was a needy thing.

Not me, though. I was prim. Proper. Rightly named Chastity.

His big rod nudged against my thigh, sending spirals of heat to the tips of my toes. Feeling its weight gave me in insatiable urge to touch it. Wrap my fingers around it. Wake him and tell him I was open to more licking.

Absolutely not. Get a grip on yourself, girl.

His tongue should be registered as a dangerous weapon. Long and thick, it was split on the tip. His highly creative tip had—

No, no, no. I needed to get out of here. I had important things to do today, things that didn't include banging hot orc construction workers for half the morning. Time was a wastin'.

Once I left this hotel room, I could slink back into my role as a respectful businesswoman who did not wear edible cherry undies, let alone ask strangers to lick them. Chew them. Rip them from her body with his tusks.

I slid out from beneath him and inched to the side of the bed. Promptly falling off the edge, I landed with a dull thud on the carpeted floor in a tangle of flushed limbs and overheated humiliation. Before my curse slipped out, I slapped my hand over my mouth and went still, listening.

He grunted but didn't move. At least he hadn't witnessed my swan dive off the bed.

Scrambling to my feet, I stood there for a second staring down at him, my heart softening at seeing his gorgeous slumbering face. The sheet had slid down to his waist, leaving his tattooed green wonderfulness exposed to my view.

Buff could be his middle name, from his washboard abs to his sculpted pecs to his chiseled-from-granite shoulders. All topped off with long black hair streaked with sunshine, a strong—now stubbly—jawline, and killer dark eyes well set in an orc-green face. It was no wonder it only took one glass of wine to make me rip off my clothing.

If I was honest with myself, something I always took pride in, he'd made me drool before I'd taken my first sip.

Snatching up my dress—a slash of conservative blue lying on the floor—my purse, and my impractical, three-inch heels I'd boldly worn the night before, I tiptoed into the bathroom and shut the door.

After flicking on the light, I glanced in the mirror, my breathing coming to a shuddering halt. Great, great, great. My cheeks were pink, I had a freakin' hickey on my neck, my breasts were perky and swollen and still called for more action, and I had a matching hickey on my upper right thigh close to where all that licking had taken place.

Lava pooled inside me at the memory, as if the hot orc construction worker was here in the tiny room with me, sliding his fingertips along my lower back. Dipping his hand between my legs. Watching me in the mirror while he did it.

"Spread your legs wider, sweetheart," he'd commanded last night. "I want to see everything."

I'd done whatever he'd asked, and I would again if he appeared and told me to bend over the vanity.

"Stop it. Get dressed. Go get your things from your room and drive away from the scene of the crime," I whispered while struggling into my sensible white panties, which I'd tucked into my purse before donning the others. Who knew where the cherry ones had wound up. Burned to a crisp by the volcanic action between us, maybe.

I tugged my dress over my head and wrangled with the back zipper, which hot guy had pulled down with his tusks last night while I sighed and urged him on. I strapped on my heels.

There. Presentable once again. Tidy enough to ride the elevator to the ground floor and walk across the hotel lobby with my head held high.

Check that thought. Leaning over the sink, I smoothed my long, brown hair, doing my best to make it appear like a guy hadn't run his fingers through it, let alone gripped it in his fist while he rode me from behind.

My knees wobbled as I fell back into that moment. A soft moan slipped from my swollen lips. There was no denying that I looked like a wanton, *wanting* woman who'd just had the best fuck of her life. Multiple fucks, that is.

Huffing, I turned away from my reflection. As

wonderful as he was, it was time for me to step back into Chastity. I had a new life and job waiting for me, neither of which included a hot guy who made my chest ache after only one night.

I shut off the light, eased open the door, and squinted into the room. Nothing but soft snoring came from the mound under the covers.

I scurried across the carpet and slipped out the door, making sure it shut behind me with a barely discernable click.

Longing coursed through my veins, and it was all I could do not to turn and knock. Beg to be let back inside.

"No, Chastity," I hissed, collapsing against the wall beside the door. "You will not do anything like that."

Elevator. Room. Lobby. *Go!*

I raced down the hall.

I'd never see my hot orc construction worker again, which was just as well, because my heart couldn't take it.

Two weeks later, I dressed in a nice skirt and blouse, sedate heels, and pulled my hair up in a tight bun. I drove to my new job and sat in the parking lot staring at the single-story building.

Zahgorim Construction Company, the sign over the front door, said. I'd taken a job as the owner's assistant. In the paperwork he sent over a month ago, he told me to have the receptionist send me down the hall on the right when I arrived. His office was at the end. He'd explain my duties then, though I had a solid idea of what was expected of me.

I would take over the management of the company Valentine's Day Picnic. I'd handle business matters not related to the hands-on construction work. And I'd complete additional tasks as assigned.

An easy position for a woman with years of administrative assistant experience under her belt.

I couldn't wait to get started.

The receptionist waved me to the hall, and I strode up to his door. At my knock, a gruff voice inside called for me to enter.

After shutting the door to the hall, I walked across an entryway and into my new boss's corner office. Pausing, I took in the expanse of windows taking up two walls with a gorgeous view of the distant mountains. Sunlight streamed through the panels, eclipsing a tall male sitting behind an enormous desk covered with various items.

He stood and strode around the desk to greet me, and I finally got a good look at his face.

My eyes widened, and I gulped, backing into the wall as I took in the hot orc construction guy I'd slept with two weeks ago.

"I . . . You . . ." The small box of candy I'd brought as a little gift slipped from my hands.

I slapped my hand over my lipstick-clad mouth, not sure what to say.

"So, you're *Chastity*," he said in the gravelly voice that had haunted me every night since I last saw—slept— with him. The deep tone alone made me wet, but the stormy look in his dark eyes made my knees knock together. "I've wondered what to call you."

He wore a black business suit, and the first few buttons of his starched white shirt were undone to show off the muscular chest I remembered licking. The glorious dark hair with natural highlights that I'd run my fingers through half the night had been pulled back and secured with a strip of leather at the back of his neck.

This was bad news. My heart couldn't take seeing him again. He *couldn't* be my new boss!

"Yes, I . . . I'm her. Chastity Jones," I mumbled. "And you're Maxon Zahgorim, my . . ." Hell, what was I supposed to call him? My one-night stand?

"Call me Max."

"I, um, sure."

Turning toward his desk, he swept his arm out, sending everything on the polished surface flying to the floor.

His dark brooding eyes shot my way as he jerked open the top few buttons of his starched white shirt. "Lay back on the desk, sweetheart."

Get Candy For My Orc Boss Now!